Alexis
Happy Birthday - it
love me
8 years

Alexis Wagman

WHEN DOLLS TALK

When Dolls Talk Copyright © 2017 by Joel R. Dennstedt. All rights reserved. Printed in the United States of America. No part of this book may be used or reproduced in any manner whatsoever without written permission except in the case of brief quotations embodied in critical articles or reviews. For information, address author@joelrdennstedt.com

First Edition
ISBN-13:
978-1542546607
ISBN-10:
1542546605

WHEN DOLLS TALK

A COLLECTION OF SHORT HORROR STORIES

JOEL R. DENNSTEDT

DEDICATION

FOR MY BRITISH AUTHOR FANS

CHANTELLE ATKINS
GLYNIS HEATHCOTE
STEPH GRAVELL

WHEN DOLLS TALK

IN MEMORY OF BECKY

CONTENTS

Introduction 1

When Dolls Talk 3

The Town Hag 13

The Blue Raven 21

The Old Place 29

By Demons Possessed 37

The Dead Dummy 47

The Watching Man 59

That Thing Upstairs 67

The Woods Girl 77

Great Uncle Jack 85

Our Little Town 93

The Hanging Girls 101

The Hanged Man 111

Afterword 121

INTRODUCTION

A horrid world infects our own.
Few write about such sin.
But mournful dolls will make us weep.
When we by error listen.

Remembering one forsaken, filled with rage.
Nosing into witch business, bequeathed remorse.
Talking to one who shouldn't, utterly confused.

Redemption and remembrance, rewarded.
Two worlds intersect, becoming vile.
The speechless one, talking too much, dies.

Foreshadowing from a shadowed self.
A botched creation, ravenous to consume.
Thievery of the most despicable kind.

Family ties that bind, and then unwind.
Where the tale-makers go.
The horrid world that permeates, opened.

One to make you hate, too many to relate.

Terrible things dolls speak about.
We cringe, then slink away.
But watching our revulsion peak,
They talk from night 'til day.

WHEN DOLLS TALK

*C*ome closer. I don't bite.
A raspy, smoky, wicked laughter echoes from her slightly parted lips.
Sorry. A little joke of mine.
Becky was a young girl of eight, almost nine, lovely in appearance; lovely in personality.
She was a nasty little bitch.
As a younger girl of six and seven, she wore pinafores and lace. She liked to be a girl. She liked to dance and twirl. She liked her dresses to swirl. Just like that, she often thought in rhyme -until she became eight, almost nine.
Clever, what you did there.
And then she stopped, both the rhyming and the dancing; the pinafores and the lace.
At eight and almost nine she went through some kind of change. Partly a physical change, though of a minor sort, and yet something also dramatically began to transform inside her head.
Some people blamed it on the doll.
Well, they would, wouldn't they.
In reality, it was the other way around. And the time has come for a truer story to be told; the record needs to be set right at last.
Oh, I just can't bloody wait.
Rebecca West moved with her family to 888 Elm Street just three days before she was to enjoy a quiet ninth birthday celebration. Unlike most girls her age who have been extricated from their intimately familiar – and therefore habitually comfortable - place of birth, and made to move without warning into new surroundings, to seek out all new friends, and to worry about the complications of attending some new school, Rebecca – or Becky, as her old friends used to call her – found herself

quite content to be moving someplace else. A new bedroom lay in wait for her, promised almost as a bribe, though unnecessarily, and this alone she found inviting, but for Miss Rebecca West the greatest pleasure came from contemplating an entirely new and fresh beginning to her life.

She was rather disappointed by the old one.

She had always been such a good girl.

But now she felt that she had gotten off to a wrong and unintended start, and until she could make this change in domiciles and thereby enter entirely into some thoroughly new surroundings, she saw no way that she could easily retreat from a predetermined path; no way to go back and start anew. Sitting now, however, on the plump new bed in her colorful new bedroom, surrounded by the pastels of her parents' taste in younger-girl décor, she gave this decidedly pregnant moment the due consideration that it deserved. And as she came to a decision regarding her new life, looking about her rather prissy room with a disdain she had just begun to feel - rather as an artist might regard a brand new canvas: blank and ready for creation – she finally noticed the little doll sitting quietly and demurely in the corner on the floor.

Such a pretty little thing.

Yeah, that was a hell of a moment for me. And, yes I was.

Actually, the doll was unbearably beautiful, and dressed very fancily too, as if anticipating an elegant evening out or as if perhaps preparing to attend a royal ball. The pearls around her neck were stunning and seemed to accentuate the royal purple of her eyes.

Stop. You're making me blush.

The pink patches upon her cheeks actually seemed to glow with an exuberance of health. Why, she almost looked alive.

Say what?

This doll was so obviously enticing to any child's dreaming fantasy that one might well have expected Becky to be moved excessively to glee, to leap down from her too-high bed and run quickly over to dramatically embrace her new-found marvelous little toy, seeing in its welcome face the kind of sudden hospitality that would signal the warm introduction of a brand new friend, a dear companion of the most absolutely special sort - but Becky did not run over; she did not leave her bed. In fact, she rather scowled, although she was unaware of the sudden drooping in her face, and with an intensely dark consideration plastered there she let her eyes rudely intrude upon the glamorous doll's pretty, almost dainty, pristinely perfect features. Becky let her mind slowly spiral down along an imaginary whirlpool of thinking, experiencing an inexorable yet cautious, gravity-generated pull toward one tiny but solid pearl of thought, which was already irritating and ingratiating itself into the clammy mucous of her morbidly transforming brain. She did not think that she was morbid, but the idea certainly had a dankly humid air about it, emanating a thick effluence in somewhat rancid waves, and she was irresistibly attracted to the darkness of this unusually new and rather rank idea, and perhaps to the morbidity of it as well. In any case, the smile that came then to her lips was anything but genuine, and rather morbid-looking, truth be told.

The doll should have been afraid.

Not yet. Fear did not come to me just yet.

But Becky did nothing about her thought right then, except to jump down from her bed and head downstairs. She did not engage much with her folks, even in her recently abandoned life, and this maintained even though she was an only child. She did not dislike or resent her mom and dad, but also she was not overly demonstrative in the love she deigned to give them, preferring to dole it out in precious little parcels. Mostly, they were just there providing for her, and they lived in an intangibly different world from that of her own lower point of view, almost like watching parental characters in a television show inhabiting higher realms. They did eat their evening meals together, and both her mom and dad were observant enough to care about their pretty little daughter, and even perhaps to notice the subtle change when it began, but neither was acute enough to think it warranted any undue attention or importance, and they simply logged their passing observation as another milestone in their daughter's young and - til then - quite successfully navigated life.

After all, she was such a good and lovely girl.

There you go again.

And so together they ate their evening meal. They talked about their day. The parents asked Rebecca if she liked her room, and of course she really did. They asked her if she was looking forward to starting classes at her new school next day, and of course she really was. And though it seemed a little odd to Becky that they did not make mention of the doll - for she had assumed the fancy girl was their sweet and pricey housewarming concession to her recent dislocation – or even perhaps an early birthday present left nonchalantly to surprise - yet for some reason she could not adequately explain, even to herself, she too held off mentioning the well-dressed plastic girl sitting in her room. She did, however, for just a moment, roll that word *dislocation* on and off her tongue, savoring it as she might the messy piece of cherry pie dissolving currently in her mouth, not noticing the tiny bit of red saliva that spittled from the corner of her lips, and she was totally unaware when her mother quickly wiped away the tiny spot of bloody-looking drool.

Her mom thought how wonderful that Becky had so much liked her piece of store-bought pie.

As this first day turned to later evening and Rebecca returned to bed, she did not give any further consideration to that newly discovered, darkened pearl inside her brain, though it remained - irritating and ingratiating – just like the spot of red which had now stained the corner of her lips, where Becky's fingers seemed to linger in a pose of concentration as she contemplated the seemingly useless little doll. She still had not embraced the toy, and even now she regarded it suspiciously, with the same penetrating gaze a small town villager might employ when noticing a new person come to town, thinking only of the unknown being as some kind of interloping threat. She squinted at this odd perception and, having already undressed herself for bed, turned over heavily and promptly went to sleep.

And finally, I breathed out heavily my own relief.

The next morning, Becky went to school.

No one at the school suspected any difference in the pretty young girl making her debut, for the very simple reason: they did not know her. And to be fair, Becky was not exactly dramatic in her transformation. The only difference from before: she simply did not portray herself as enthusiastically social as did her former self; she did not brightly smile the other girls into friendship like before, and she did not garner the attention of the boys as actively as before. In truth, she did not consciously avoid these prior affectations; she just settled into a kind of solitary quiet that let her swim among the schooling kids like a barely noticed fish stuck in the middle of an enormous swirling pod. A few kids, the ones with studded lips and noses and piercings in unusual places, would sometimes feel compelled to glance her way, but then they would wonder what had drawn their attention and immediately look away.

Thus, this newer Becky went quietly unremarked.

And later she came home.

Often placed – unresentfully on her part - into the role of a latch-key kid, like today, she made herself a snack and climbed with it up the stairs, where she went into her bedroom and sat upon the bed and thought about her day. She felt herself to be in somewhat of a mood, an atypical occurrence for her, as she was usually quite content to daydream, read a book, watch TV, or play with any of her many games, perhaps even a semi-electronic toy. As she munched upon a cookie, she contemplated the unsettled nature of her stomach, and eventually she came to a most surprising, disturbing, and reluctant conclusion: she felt angry. Rebecca was not a child prone to anger, so she had not recognized the early symptoms. But, yes, she definitely felt anger in her stomach now. And just when she decided there was absolutely no reason for this distressing feeling, she caught her pretty doll staring up at her from the floor. Staring at her most insolently, as a matter of actual fact. She frowned, and the frown turned into a challenge.

"What are you staring at, you dumb mute freak?"

To her credit, she was startled by this sudden and crudely stated exclamation.

And yet...it felt rather good to call the doll a dirty name.

"You dumb mother-fu..." but she clasped her hand quickly to her mouth in stark surprise and quick revulsion at the venom in her voice. Still, unbelievably she thought: that felt really good, and it had made her giggle at her own rudely executed verbal outburst. Still, the dolly only stared. Which seemed somehow to fuel her newly aroused and now eager-to-be-unleashed virulent anger, and she let loose a stream of vile invectives with the explosive force of sickness, spewing epithets and curses like a champ, as if expelling all the vileness from a place of illness deep inside her belly. Totally exhausted, the relief she felt was utterly invigorating. She thought the doll's eyes had actually widened, perhaps in terror at her fury, though rationally she knew that it must be only her imagination. That consideration made her giggle yet again, which this time – contrarily - came out as a sort of evil cackle, sounding too much like a sniveling witch, and she could swear the plastic creature let out a hopeless, if suppressed, tiny little moan.

I couldn't help myself.

And this croaking sign of abject surrender to a helpless vulnerability is what finally got Becky off her bed and crouching on her knees before the staring little doll, whose widely open eyes now seemed to convey a bit of panic and concern, not to mention the atavistic fear of any timid creature who has unwittingly been noticed by one who might severely do them harm.

Becky plucked at and fidgeted with the fabric of the doll's formal fancy dress, rubbing the parchment dryness of its brittle lacy cloth between her thumb and finger, musing as she did so on the little ruby brooch fastened just beneath the pearl necklace encircling the dress's high-necked collar. "Too good for you," she murmured, but left the ornaments alone. Instead, she continued fingering the sleeves and hems as if she might suddenly rip them from the idle plastic body; she had that foreboding sense of catastrophe quivering in her calm, intrusive touch. "I wonder if you have a name," she whispered, as if sharing some dark secret.

I did not. Not then. Not like the cursed one that I share now.

"You would make a perfect little Becky," Becky said.

And then, as if inflicted with an explosive inspiration, she conclusively announced, "We need to make you up!"

And up she stood.

Then she ran into her mother's room, which she had never intruded upon before when home alone, and she looked around as if she had entered a magical new realm, standing there in awe looking at all of the big girl furnishings – especially at the table with the mirror and the lights, and the shiny metallic casings lined up like little soldiers, and the little pastel boxes, and the many brushes and other unknown and mysterious accoutrements all waiting patiently to be used. But none of this was what she wanted.

So, down the stairs she went.

Where, in a tiny closet beside the kitchen, sitting quite recently unused - because the house was new and clean – she located her mom's old vacuum cleaner, the one she absolutely knew must contain a bag filled to the brim with dust and hairs and unmentionable debris from their recently vacated and very dirty home.

No surprise there; she was not to be disappointed.

What she collected she put inside a bowl, but knowing she still lacked something vital to her needs, she plopped herself down at the kitchen table to ponder her next move. And looking at the small back door leading to the garage, she had a further brainstorm: she would rummage. That is what her father did: he rummaged in the garage, and though she held no particular love for her father, he did seem always to find the things he needed, and he found them just by rummaging around.

So that is what she did.

Where, by great good fortune, she found precisely what she needed, in a thickly folded bag, scrunched in upon itself on the chilly cement floor, beneath the small wooden workbench where her dad would sometimes putter after rummaging around. Reaching deep into the blue and red and white thick bag with the barbecue picture on the front – where some goofy, grinning thin man in an apron and a chef's hat posed as if cooking something on a grill – she extricated a single charcoal briquette and admired the smoky dust it left immediately powdered upon her hand. "Perfect," she whispered to herself, as pleased and glowing with anticipation as if she were to celebrate her birthday on this day rather than the next.

With the small briquette held firmly and securely in her fist, she returned into the kitchen, grabbed the bowl of hairy dust, and fairly flew back up the stairs into her private bedroom, being sure to close the door behind her, and then turning deliberately around with a deeply scowling squint upon her face as she stared at that insolent little doll.

"I'll show you," she croaked.

And for the next hour and a half, as so many little girls do, she proceeded to apply make-up to her doll – her little Becky.

I shall never be the same.

Later, she thoroughly washed her hands and descended to the main room to wait for mom and dad, to join them both for dinner at the table, to talk about her day at school, and to tell them just how much she was looking forward to her birthday.

They could not have been more pleased with their precious little girl, who actually seemed to be warming up to them at last. They were not overly surprised when she excused herself early after eating and headed to her room. They wrote it off to her excitement about tomorrow, and of course, her love for her new bedroom.

"She must really like the way you did her room," observed her dad.

"I know. Isn't it great?" her mom agreed.

And they turned their rapt attention back to the television show that they were watching and laughing at together on the couch.

One of them hummed a little in her contentment.

Upstairs, Rebecca stared relentlessly at her precious little doll.

Her loving gaze wandered lingeringly over the heavily soiled, lacy dress, looking now like something from some dusty old museum, a place where ancient artifacts collected age like mementos from a distant time, with bits of hair and clotted stuff protruding from the tiny spaces created within the lace, and she admired the ghastly brittle hair that now sprung from dolly's head like some discarded rag, and was even gapped to baldness where small clusters had been patiently, persistently wrenched out, and she had even managed to expertly create a network of shattered little cracks upon her face – like tiny veins that had exploded beneath the plastic skin – by using the kitchen bowl just like a hammer, cracking at that pernicious face with careful, repetitious blows, until it just looked so perfect she could cry, but then the eyes....oh yes, the eyes: they were an absolute masterpiece of decorating skill. Becky actually giggled with heartfelt glee at what she had done all around little Becky's purple orbs using just the powder from the dark briquette. Some might call it a raccoon look, but Becky called it haunted. And as she stared, she basked in the sound and flavor of that beautiful, singular sounding word: *haunted*.

There was only one thing left to do.

She broke the dolly's leg.

I did not scream. I did not give her that satisfaction. But I could not stop the tear. I just could not.

When Becky saw the single drop of liquid fall from little Becky's eye, she was nothing short of ecstatic. She whispered huskily, like an older woman at her peak of pleasure, "Oh, yes!" And then she said, "I knew it."

And she broke the other leg.

The next morning, when Becky's mom came up to wake her sleepy-headed birthday girl, she found her dead upon the floor, her dress in disarray, her hair splayed like some old rag, her face shattered like a vase, her legs twisted from her body like broken sticks...and yes, her eyes: oh, her eyes were just so very *haunted*.

Well, I just had to, didn't I.

THE END

THE TOWN HAG

I am a young man living in a village outside of time. What I mean: our township is not within your world; not your time, not your place, not your life. You might recognize it as a European village just prior to the industrial rise of concentrated cities – a rural town, secluded, near a forest and a river and a vast expanse of vacant land, a home for people who make their living from the industrious working of the land; farmers, if that makes you feel more comfortable. I am myself a worksmith, a title denoting one who does errands for other folks. I run around the village - and to the farther outlying homes - delivering things and fixing others, telling folks what other folks apparently need urgently to know.

I get around.

Right now, I am running an errand for the blacksmith. I assume you know what work he does. The time of day is later in the afternoon, or early in the evening; in either case the sky is dimming as I run about my business. My particular chore today has me running along the outskirts of the Field; it is simply called the Field, for that in truth is all it is. Not only is the sky dimming into dusky gray, but the wind is picking up, the birds are whisking urgently about, and there is that hollow feeling in the air that one notices when things are feeling not quite right. You know what I mean.

I am not discomfited by the feeling – I like when things remain a bit off-kilter or out-of-synch; it makes me feel as if the world has temporarily shifted on its axis and maybe, somewhere, a breech in its everyday reality has occurred – but I do become more aware and specifically alert to whatever may find its errant way into the breech, thereby slinking its temporary way into our world. I'm not sure why I think of things quite like that. But I do. For I have definitely seen some things.

Like today, as I am running by the Field, I see amongst the wavering, stalk-like weeds - beneath the dimming sky and fractious birds - the hunchbacked figure of an obviously ancient woman making her way slowly across the vacant land, all shawled up with heavy skirts, wearing a thick and wooly cloak, with a separate shawl covering her head and shading the features of her face, her eyes lost within her self-created shadows, a gnarled wooden cane held out before her like a blind man's, her movements like a crone.

She is the local hag, the one who by her strangeness defines our displaced little town.

She certainly isn't the blonde girl of my dreams; the one I still have yet to meet.

I have seen our hag only once or twice before, on other days like today, but I don't know if she just comes rambling her way in through the breech, or if she prefers such oddly manifesting weather for removing herself from a slyly hidden dwelling and mincing her way into town. I have not seen from whence she comes; she usually just appears. She makes her huddled, secretive, and painful way from alleyway to alley, approaching shops only from the back to buy her wares; never talking, always stalking, moving stealthily – almost warily - from shadow into shadow. By such mystery of movement has she caught my eye and made me wonder, for I have been plotting out a plan inside my curious head to find her out.

That is why I stop to watch her stumble on her way across the empty field.

She has come late into town today; she will not be leaving before dark. I shall bide my time, and finish up my chores. Then I shall return and stake out a spot from which to watch for her return, and I shall follow - dark or not - and I shall find out where she lives.

*****

I must have dozed. From my hiding place behind the potter's shed, I look out into the dark where I know the Field to be, and I see a bobbing light making its way slowly along the empty furrows, moving farther away from where I sit. I know that it can only be the hag returning home. I get up to follow, quickly brushing off my pants and brushing back my hair with the fingers of one hand - I don't know why; just a habit thing, I guess.

Trampling over the crumbled terrain of a field left to fallow is an extremely difficult and physically arduous task. Even in the light of day it is hard to keep one's balance; in the dark, it is downright impossible. And, as is rather a typical thing for me, I admit: I have been a bit precipitous in my urge to follow the old hag, neglecting in my haste and lack of thought to provide myself with a lantern or a torch by which to find my way should I lose the rapidly diminishing light flickering its way now into the forest. I share a bit of moonlight from the sliver that is new, but it serves only to silhouette the trees toward which I am determinedly heading, and to mark their barricading border with the Field.

This lumbering trek of mine across the languishing furrows makes me feel like I have recently indulged in too much raucous drinking at the tavern, but surely if I had been besotted by over-drinking, by now I would have planted my earnest face somewhere in the weedy, clotted dirt. Instead, I simply stagger as if I might be drunk in pursuit of that ever bobbing light shining singly far up ahead - a tiny, hiccupping beacon in the night – which is now disappearing almost completely as it enters into the denser woods. I must make haste if I am not to lose my way.

I am able to make it to the trees, and there I sense what seems to be a slight trail leading through the woods, but I must rely upon my feet to find my way, for the moon has been eclipsed by the canopy of treetops overhead, and the witch's feeble light – I should not call her that; it is a mark of disrespect; I should be more watchful of my tongue, and my thoughts as well – shows only momentary glimpses like a single firefly in the night. I strain to keep the little moving star in sight, for only by its flickering do I know which way to go. God help me if any real fireflies should suddenly appear and decide to flit about, especially if they disperse in separate ways.

*****

I am staring at what looks to be a wooden lodge or cabin settled deep amongst the trees. A light is glowing dimly from inside, but one could be forgiven if he did not recognize this as someone's personal abode – it seems to be a displaced vision, maybe from the other side of the breech, or at least from some storyteller's more vibrant imagination. Something about it does not ring true, but perhaps – once again – that is just a perceptual fault of mine. I am ever careful to walk quietly as I approach the dwelling, anxious that the wi... hag does not hear me blundering about outside and errantly think that I am a prowler. Or even worse, a thief. I am not here to startle or alarm her. I am merely and pertinaciously curious.

And so, quite tentatively, I peek inside the window.

I do not see anyone at home.

I crane my neck, stretching all around to see the whole interior, for the hag must have made it home before me, but it is just a small place and therefore easily and quickly scanned; I see that it is quite cluttered all about with knickknacks, trinkets, baubles, gimcracks, and other gewgaws – the trifles that make a home comfortable for a loner - with so much stuff scattered everywhere on shelves and counters, chairs and tables, I cannot imagine where the old crone sits, much less sleeps. I am mesmerized by the mess. But, where then can the old hag be?

Startled, I quickly look around, afraid a bony finger may soon peck angrily at my shoulder or jab into my neck, but there is only darkness in what might be called the yard, a severely limited, hardscrabble area, and rather vacant too, similar to the Field. Glancing at the front door of the cabin, I notice a thinly outlined vertical crevice limned with light, and I know the door is cracked partly open - as if the dwelling were intended to be closed but left behind for only a short while.

The invitation is simply irresistible.

Once inside, I stop and look around again, as if by chance my eyes have missed the hag sitting somewhere within all that clutter, herself looking perchance like some antiquated gewgaw lost amongst the rest. But the only thing that I have missed is the small closet situated by the front door, its own door open but a crack as well, wherein I must assume there only sits a broom and perhaps also is hung the hag's dark cloak and shawl. My curiosity is piqued – an ironic phrase, considering the events which are soon to follow – and, like a cat, I let curiosity draw me into the single room that bespeaks the entirety of that rather claustrophobic place. My eyes linger on the curios scattered all about, fastening especially and intently on the doo-dads in the kitchen, which are sitting on the counter like unwashed dishes, but looking more like pieces of the laboratory apparatus used by our pharmacists in the town: tiny ceramic pots and bowls, measuring tubes and stirring sticks, colored-glassware beakers and fluted flasks – all looking somewhat the worse for wear, as if allowed to become a breeding spot for fungi and for mold; creating a cloudy and besmirching veil of murky and effluent grime to hide the originally pristine stone and glass – all of which conveys to me a decidedly mysterious concern for some kind of obsessive preoccupation, leading me to ask myself: what in the world could she be doing here?

I hear a graveled cough come from somewhere quite nearby outside, and for the first time in my life I hear the old woman speak: "Get in yar, ya damn cat."

The sound she makes is ghastly; it rasps like grit upon the ear, and at first I freeze in reaction to the sudden fear that such a sound automatically invokes within the human frame, but gathering my wits quickly, I fairly leap into the closet. Regrettably, I realize that I may have thoughtlessly just sealed my fate, for now I shall likely be found hiding rather than simply waiting for a visit, as lame as that would sound as an excuse for my bold intrusion. In fact, I might have just made my own bed – as the elders are prone to say – and here it is I might have to sleep this dismal night away, a victim once again of my precipitously active nature. For now, I must control my breathing, and hunker down behind her shawl and cloak, and hope their presence here denotes no further need for additional access to the closet. I leave the door cracked open, in case she possesses an attentive kind of soul and notices the change.

She kicks the cat into the room, and closes the door behind her.

And through the crack I watch her pause and sniff the air around her.

She seems to chuckle then, and to mumble some little incantatory admonition to herself, as if she has absentmindedly left something cooking and unattended on the stove. She even executes a twisted little jig, which oddly makes me feel self-conscious and ashamed by my unintended privacy invasion and my witnessing of such an embarrassingly self-indulgent act.

I lean back into the closet wall, pretending not to notice.

I am still sitting all scrunched up and somewhat huddled upon the floor of this crampy, confining closet, yearning mightily to stretch my quickly stiffening limbs, when I see the golden eyes of her scrawny, scraggly cat peering at me through the crevice in the door, suddenly seeing what he has heretofore only sensed. Himself startled, he lets out a sudden, terrifying hiss, and prepares himself to howl, when the hag impatiently yanks the small door open, kicks the cat inside, and slams the shaky old door closed, never noticing me sitting here on the floor, in the dark, behind the cloak and shawl. We are together in the dark, the cat and I, and he now begins to yowl unmercifully, at which the hag screeches him toward silence, followed immediately by some archly arcane threat, both of which the cat ignores, until I must reach out and unfortunately grasp him by the neck.

If you've ever held a cat unwilling, you know why I must kill him.

I did not plan this. I must do it to shut him up.

Which seems to satisfy the hag, who goes happily about her business unawares.

Since curiosity looms its head once more - after taking proper care of the cat - I am bold enough to crack the door open once again, just a little, and I peek out into the room.

She is busy at the sink.

But she is not washing up the dishes.

She seems to be puttering about.

I do wonder how I shall ever make what must be a stealthy exit, but for now I remain reluctantly constrained to watching her strange ambulations amongst the various clutterings in the room. She picks up little things from here and there and takes them to the sink. She pours a variety of smelly fluids from small containers into beakers, and also into those maleficently-hued and crusty flasks. She lights up some kind of miniaturized burner-rod, and brings the fluids to a boil. She is quite encapsulated in her laboratorial world, and, I truly hate to say it, but she looks just like a witch. Even as I think the thought, she cackles.

After a while, she begins singing to herself, or to the uncritical and captive audience that haunts the interior of the room, but I soon realize that she is not so much singing as she is incanting, exactly as a witch might incantanize her brew. Somehow, this disturbs me most of all.

I really want to leave.

Instead, I sit back down as I prepare myself for a long, uncomfortable, and very tiresome evening.

*****

I must have dozed again. The room is dark. Not just inside the closet, because the door crack shows no light intruding from without. I shift a little, trying desperately to remain quiet, and of course I plop my hand into the furry softness of the soon to be long-dead cat. God, I hope she did not love that cat. I assume I must take it with me to dispose of it somewhere else. Let her wonder where her source of small delight took off to.

I wonder where she is.

But as I crack the closet door open even more, I can hear her snoring somewhere across the room. I assume she is lying on the couch - after putting the clutter somewhere else. At least I hope, because I am headed out the front door with as much speed and as little noise as I can muster; dead cat well in tow.

The first glow of morning greets me at the door. I need to empty my bladder badly, and at the first large tree I drop the cat and take care of nature's business. My relief is almost as sublime as escaping from that dark closet. I have no desire to carry the cat any farther, so I leave it by the tree and make my grand retreat. The hag can simply wonder at her cat's mysterious demise, not to mention how it may have made its way out of the closet and then, even stranger, managed to open up the front door. Ah well, it may distract her from considering a possible intruder in the night. As for me, my curiosity is not satisfied, but it certainly is gone. I have no further wish to know any more about the hag. She is much too strange and scary for this young man's temperament, and besides, I am feeling guilty about the cat. I would dearly like to put this evening and the hag and her strange dwelling far behind me; perhaps forget about them altogether.

As I make my way back across the Field, I do feel a kind of normalcy returning. There is no wind; no agitated birds crashing about a dissipated sky. The morning air is fresh and crisp, and I find myself yearning for some coffee and some eggs, and later perhaps a reconstructive nap to soothe my weary bones. I think about the rashness of my decision yesterday to follow the town hag, and I can only pawn my motivation off on the strangeness of the day – the kind of day when the world might be breeched and an oddness might begin to flavor the atmosphere all around. On such a day I seem always to make a somewhat regrettable decision to investigate what other times would not really be all that bizarre.

I thought it so important to investigate the hag, to follow her and to find her hidden home; to discover more of who she is.

Not today. Today, she is just another too-old woman living by herself. A woman without a cat, but perhaps she'll find another. I do not consider this my problem anymore. My problem is to find some eggs and coffee. My problem will then be to secure myself a nap.

*****

I must have dozed.

When I awaken, in a pile of straw beside the blacksmith's, near the corral where cows are kept, I yawn and stretch and greet the sunny day that probably rests somewhere right near noon. I feel better, if not totally refreshed, and my memory of the night before feels rather like a dream. I suppose I must seek out my chores, and after brushing off my clothes and stroking back my hair – habitual grooming taken care of – I head off down the alley toward the main street, where I pause to scrutinize the passing people.

Not far down the street I see: the blond girl of my dreams.

THE END

THE BLUE RAVEN

*B*loody Poe.
He ruined it for us all.
We all know it now: the man was quite insane; wacko to the core. Some asshole of a raven comes knocking at his window, only to croak one word in repetition – lord, if the man had not already been insane, that alone would surely have made him jump from the nearest looney-bin's highest rooftop. Apparently, the drugs had ill-prepared him for the visitation. And now I know it must be fact – it must have really happened, though he tried to pawn it off on Dickens - because with me it was a dark blue raven who came calling in the faded light of a waning day, and his long and garbled message meant specifically for my attention was certainly more than just a single, nastily spoken word. Hell, I couldn't shut the damn bird up. *Not ever*, to paraphrase the Master. And if one word can drive you nuts, just think how an entire message might infiltrate your brain and insinuate itself within your worst, self-considered thoughts, and then, what might be the mental consequences of having such a terrible intruder ensconced so deeply in your mind?

For the message was the problem; not just the insane appearance of that really annoying and chatty bird – obnoxious, belligerent, and provocative as he proved himself to be.

Suppose I tell you what he said?

I shall try to circle 'round it first, but don't thank me yet for such considerate circumspection. And before I do, maybe I should tell you how I came to be here, in this queer distorted little house in the center of this cozy, patriotic town, home at times to many of the finest founding fathers, writers almost every one, and smart too, like the great old man who died here - in the city, not the house – leaving behind so many little sayings of gentle wisdom that there is an almanac written in his name; well, not his specific name, but the name of someone he invented.

But I digress and ramble.

I do that now.

A lot.

I came into this quaintly-thought-of-city on my own quite some time ago. I don't recall how long it's been now; perhaps more than one full year. Where I came from, I also do not recall, and if you find that just the tad bit disconcerting, try thinking about how I must feel. As if I had harkened fully grown from some otherworldly existence shrouded by a foggy cloud defined by things-not-quite-real into this picturesque community of fraternal pride and oft' repeated anecdotal history.

I am a poet.

It's a condition; Frost said so.

And maybe that is why I was drawn to this house: it suits my poetic disposition.

Standing on a leaf-strewn autumn sidewalk, bundled against the crisp fall air, I found myself looking longingly at it from across the shady street, where I was taken by the charm of its old-world splendor and personality. Yes, it was distorted somewhat by the history of its age, giving one the optical illusion of a building leaning only slightly to one side, but that may have been but the effect given to it by its standing up so regally tall and narrow, with several separate rooftops forming acutely angled triangles leading upward into the blustery cloudy sky - like modern rockets waiting ever so patiently to launch. And near the very top, embedded in one small and isolated cupola, a tiny window dark and dreary beckoned – as if cooing down to me; wooing me from its perch on high.

"Come on up then; write something," it seemed to whisper.

To my somewhat startled delight and fond surprise, another window on the main floor - right next to the entry door - also beckoned, but this time with a written invitation: Room for Rent – and I just knew that it must be the one calling me from up on high, the one I claimed already to be mine. I had money in my pocket, a quaint surprise as well. I did not hesitate to use it toward securing my occupancy rights, although the landlady of the house – a rather lackluster human being; nice enough, I guess, just not one nearly as enamored of the place as I – was reluctant to accompany me to my room, whether from a sense of decorum, laziness, or simply disinclination, I could not say, but she did not seem unduly put out or distressed by my obvious lack of personal possessions – perhaps she thought I might retrieve them later, which of course I did not do, having none of which I knew, nor in the fuzziness of my recall, not knowing where they might reside; in any case, right then and there, I took up living in my little tower room.

But again, I ramble.

Her last words to me before leaving: "No smoking in the room." Followed by a little nod toward an inordinately narrow door, which I assumed to be a cupboard closet, and the remainder of her admonition: "Take the stairs."

I had a bed. I had a table. Oddly, on the table there was an inkwell with a well-nibbed pen and an ordered pile of blank white paper. *Convenient*, I thought, as I wandered over to the tower window to look down at where I had been standing while observing and feeling so enamored of that same small window from my secluded spot below. I could see the shady, leaf-strewn sidewalk where I had stood, but raising my eyes to take in a much larger view, I could not make out anything by looking outward toward the city – the buildings I knew to be there were only murky smudges against the fog, like errant worn splotches on a poorly cared for painting, and I figured I would need to wait for the further clearing of the day before I might see more.

I must have returned then to the table and begun writing poetry with that fine-nibbed pen and midnight-blue ink, for when next I took notice for my surroundings, a great deal of the paper pile had been whittled down, and in its place – on the other side of the table – lay a well-scratched compendium of poetic verse. Feeling quite satisfied with myself, yet rather oblivious to having yet again endured the creative process, I sat back in the chair and noticed that the day outside was beginning to turn a darker gray, not from a thickening of the fog, but because the day was simply waning into evening. And, contrary to any awareness of such a particular form of habitual surcease, I found that I suddenly wanted very much to smoke.

Patting my pocket like a true devotee of sin, I was both surprised and not to find a pack of smokes contained therein. I had no doubt that when I stood up I would find a lighter in my right pants pocket. Remembering the words of my departing hostess, and yet, almost by familiar habit too, I opened up the uncommonly narrow cupboard-closet door, and - as if by chance - I found a circular stairwell spiraling sharply down. Sliding my extended fingers along the cool, confining, curving wall, as if to maintain my balance, I descended. I circled around many times before reaching the ground floor, so I was a little disoriented as to my exact location when I encountered the narrow wooden door located at the bottom. Upon opening it, however, I was not surprised to find myself entering an outdoor garden – a very small garden, enclosed along one side by the large house wall, and on the others by rather high hedges left untrimmed but neatly fitted to the squareness of the area. Small shrubberies and dead stems – or simply dormant plants, which I assumed would blossom again in spring – footed the hedges, while a small lawn of sorts provided a soft and silent carpet underfoot. Of course, what caught my eye immediately was the concrete table sitting directly in the middle of the yard, with its circular top overlooked by the leafy branches of an umbrella-like tree beside it, and with a singular – possibly uncomfortable – iron trellised chair awaiting my immediate disposition.

The tree leaves rustled a bit as I sat down, as if to acknowledge the primacy of my presence. I loved this part of autumn: how the crispness of a fawning breeze could seem almost friendly in its greeting. And how an autumn smoke could invigorate the poet's soul. I lit my cigarette and took an exploratory drag, leaning back into my chair and tipping it farther in that direction for a somewhat appropriate if parlous sense of relaxation. I blew my smoke into the air to add my own minor contribution to the haze, took a second, deeper drag, and folded myself further into the coziness of my thickly padded coat – an accoutrement I must have unconsciously acquired – and sat thus companionably with the pleasant warmth of my own unencumbered thoughts.

The garden was quiet.
Peaceful.
Like a cemetery may be peaceful.
It was still evening; not dark. The sky was dim, but still glowed with that inner light so typical of fall. The breeze rustled still; the tree seemingly vibrantly alive with the somewhat macabre spirit of the season, almost as if it might begin to speak

of portents yet to come, with apocalyptic visions thereafter sure to follow. I could have had a coherent interaction with that tree, had the raven not suddenly appeared, asserting himself and dominating any further imagined conversation. He came out of the foggy grayness, fluttering down to land precisely on the table rim, as if showing off his skills, yet keeping his head directed forward - as if there in the near distance lay his truer interest – which only served to keep his single oily eye affixed on me like a declaration or a challenge.

He was hunched over slightly, as if burdened by his heavy shoulders.

The feathers of his craw were ruffled, as if to clear a congested throat.

His beak was long and sharply curved, and darker than his feathers, which were all a cobalt shade of blue. A blue raven: something I had never seen or thought to possibly imagine. Sitting on the table edge, staring arrogantly into my face. I don't know why, but I had the impression that he was antsy and disgruntled, or at least somehow displeased to be there – like it was some kind of avian obligation to which he had been unkindly driven, like maybe I was somehow supposed to acknowledge his unique appearance at my side, and maybe even thank him. But all he said was, "Hey."

As a poet, my surprise was mitigated by classic precedence.

When, however, I did not respond, he did a little shuffle step with his feet and turned to face me, cocking his head a little bit to the side as if to ask perhaps if I were daft. But his nod was for my cigarette burning idly between my fingers, and with that little nod, he croaked, "Share a smoke?" The raspiness of his voice, although common to a crow, sounded like he might have indulged the nasty habit far too long himself, a warning to the threat implied. Still mute, I did extend the smoke, upon which he clasped his open beak and drew in a lung-filling breath that would do a large man proud, seeming to savor it a while, then without so much as a hint that he might be inclined to cough, he exhaled the smoke into the air with the hiss so revelatory of such refined contentment.

"Thanks," he said.

Then and there, the interrogation began.

"What're you doin' here, mate?"

"I beg your pardon?" I said.

"Easy question," he said. "Did I stutter?"

"Wouldn't have a flask on ya, would ya?" he added.

It seemed like an appropriate question to ask at that point, but it wasn't the one I answered.

"I write poetry," I said.

"No bloody shit," he croaked. "I kinda figured it. But why here, doof?"

"Here?"

He did a funny thing then with his outstretched wing, fluttering it violently as if trying to make the dramatic gesture that would encompass all of our surroundings.

"This place," he croaked.

I pondered on that a bit.

"It's where I might do some work," I offered, unconvincingly. As if to embellish the explanation, I added, "It has a certain ambience."

The raven quirked his head and seemed to regard me queerly, that one oily eye of his filled with something I chose not to define precisely, but it was not softly kind in its sense of wonder, and obviously, though reluctantly, held at bay some harshly unkind judgement.

"Where, exactly, do you think you are?" he asked.

"What do you mean?"

"Simple question."

But it did not seem simple to my mind. I looked around, and it was easy to describe my immediate surroundings, and even to relate in some detail the furnishings of my room, as well as the placement of this old, Victorian-style house within the city, that famous - colonially and historically - important town. And yet, unremembering of my time prior to coming here, it was difficult to provide the necessary context of my arrival, and therefore difficult to say, exactly, where I thought I was right then. The raven, sensing my discomfort, waved it off – so to speak – with another ruffling of his feathers and a hunching of his heavy shoulders.

"Forget it," he said. "Who are you, then?"

"What?"

"You heard me well enough, I think."

Our ragged conversation had begun to be annoying. The haughty manner of his attitude began to bug me; the impertinence of his assumptive questioning had gotten on my nerves – and I was highly disconcerted to find myself searching for what were unrecoverable answers.

"I told you: I am a poet," I said.

"Not the question I asked," he retorted. "Give me a name."

Try as I might, I could not. The hazy smoke from my cigarette, the mildly undulating fog drifting just beyond the walls, the deeper fog farther toward the city: all might have been the dreary haze lodged inside my brain – for all the good my inner eyes were able to discern the distinct patterns of my own shape.

"I cannot," said I, finally. And then, as if the croaking creature standing right before me might possess the answer, I asked, "What is wrong with me?"

At that, he shuffled slightly on his scrawny talons, doing a little sideways hop-step, looking at me severely, as if preparing me for his message.

"I can tell you," he said, "but you must ponder on it a while. You must let it sink inside your bones, and face the answer as the prey does his own predatory fate. But first, I must ask you one more question: do you remember her?"

"Her?"

His head nodded, though whether in affirmation or just a quirk peculiar to his breed, I could not tell.

"The one you loved," he said, though offering no more than that.

And somewhere in that foggy haze, I saw a form – no more.

The figure of a woman; the surging feeling of love and hope – then no more.

"Almost," I whispered, as the form began to fade.

"Then I must tell you," this bird of blue croaked in a sadder tone of voice. "You let her go, when you must not. You let her fade away. You spoke your self-inflicted words of hurt; she took her own way out. You sought to find her, but where she went, no living man may go. You saw her – no more."

"No more," I echoed, in a truly hollow tone of voice.

"Her memory too," he said, forlorn.

After that, we sat in silence for a while. What else was there to do?

When darkness came at last, I rose up from the table and prepared to find elusive solace in my room – solace for the memory no longer mine.

"I am not finished," croaked the raven.

And then, I swear, he preened himself as if about to make some grand entry upon a stage, strutting forward and coming to stand square and center beneath a non-existent spotlight, there to make his soliloquy of a speech, which, after pausing for the dramatic, tension-producing effect, he began.

"When you find yourself weak and weary, alone there in your room, trying to write your poetry, but remembering only my dark, foreboding words, remember this: you are not where you think you are; you are not who you think you are."

And with that most cryptic message, he was gone. I did not see him fly away. I simply saw him there – no more.

I returned to the sanctity of my little tower room, and I stared out into the darkness of the night. I thought about the words of that aggravating bird; I thought about the message he had given me; I thought about the memories that would not come, but mostly I just sat and stared and thought: I am not where I think I am; I am not who I think I am.

Every morning after that encounter found me standing there the same, staring into the foggy light of day, searching for a figure I could never see, trying to remember the origin of my birth, the story of my life, the point at which I had chosen to come into this city and occupy this tower room – to write my endless poems. Only once did I catch a glimpse of something else, actually a sound. Down in the streets beyond my own, I heard a siren wail, and I was captured by the plaintive cry of one eternal soul alone like me. And in my head, I knew the siren issued from a pure white van – an emergency vehicle headed directly for its own healing haven, to the only place its wailing siren might be calmed.

And plastered on the white van door – an emblem embossed in blue.

THE END

THE OLD PLACE

When Walter decided to return to the old place, he did not make the decision easily. Although many years had passed, the memories were still strong. He was not certain that he could return to a place with such bad feelings, but something – someone - was calling to him; something or someone who dearly, almost desperately, wanted – needed – him to return. And he never had been capable of ignoring such raw, unbridled need. Therefore, with a reluctance bordering on anathema, Walter headed home.

His trek back was long, as he had relocated – purposefully – far away from that dark, secluded house of younger days. Even as he walked deep into forgotten lands on a dismal, dank, and rutted road that led – eventually – to the starkly singular dwelling in the woods, he felt the foggy darkness getting dimmer, the air becoming more thickly humid, and his own oppressive thoughts growing ever more stifling with admonitory warning, and though he knew the house to be deserted – no one could bear the imbued weight of such vile memories that would always haunt and possess that old, abandoned homestead – he also knew that, at least for him, the house could never be considered truly empty.

He saw the building first as just a boxlike silhouette situated in the fog, ensconced within the grasp of several gnarled, long-dead tree trunks, with their wispy lacework of spidery long-dead limbs, as if the house had been seduced into the sticky grasp of a gigantic spider's web, and held there – ignored and quite forgotten – for eons of passing years. When Walter had been a family member living there, with the mom and dad and younger girl, the old place had looked and felt the same: like an insect's desiccated carapace abandoned by a monstrous spider who had sucked the insect dry.

And yet, a family lived inside.

His family.

Approaching the old place now, Walter shivered and sniffed the air outside, as if to identify by smell the rancid recollections collecting all around him like the myriad of flies that used to gather in the yard – meaningless and useless, simply drawn to that spot by association with the morbidity of rottenness, decay, and death.

He really should not have come.

And yet, that call.

So now he circled carefully around and toward the rear, making his way gingerly through the raggedy undergrowth and muck, through the matted leaves and clinging vines, through the musty earth and past the rotted logs, across the fly-infested field, to the little door in back – where he pushed his way inside.

The mustiness was overwhelming, and it made him sneeze.

And though the house was mostly cast in darkness - the dim light outside the windows making of them a group of suggested lighter rectangles in the room - he knew his way around. He wandered for a while, though not venturing up the stairs, but only to confirm his first impression that no one lived here anymore. Although he knew the placatory but commanding call had come from this location – something he sensed with an immediate and absolute certainty – the call had not been made from something – someone – in current residence. The house itself was dead. As if embalmed by morticians from an ancient time, the interior of the old place was shrouded about with layered cobwebbed swathing, and inundated with heavy sediments of clinging dust and mold and dirt. A place not just dead, but decaying quickly into the oblivion of age. A place forgotten and rejected; decidedly abandoned, clearly without remorse, regret, or recollection.

Except...Walter did recall.

And as he found for himself a somewhat untouched corner in which to curl up and wait – for he knew the caller must eventually appear – those memories he had buried for so long came now to populate the house; to fill the vacant rooms with the apparitions of the past, and to fill up Walter's senses – after so many idle, senseless years – with his family once again.

Upon recalling them, he whimpered.

Kathy appeared there first – the little girl – looking as she had when she had first come into his life; when she had found him in the woods, shaking from fear and hunger, and had wrapped him up snugly in the rags that were her only dress. She had brought him home. Into this very kitchen room that was also a poor man's parlor, tucking him into perhaps this precise secluded corner in a pile of dirty rags, then begging the stern – no, rock hard, violent man that was her father – to please allow her to keep and feed and love him. And perhaps his very harmlessness – his absolute helplessness before the world – convinced that monster of a man to tell his daughter *yes*. For even then, Walter had seen the look that told him this man would always be the determiner of his final fate.

And the little girl would be his savior.

Before their roles became reversed.

Walter grew up quickly, though he learned and was thoroughly conditioned early on to avoid the master's boot. The little girl, Kathy, did not: either grow up much at all during his own maturing year, or ever learn how to avoid her father's wrath, which was sudden and explosive. In their more intimate moments when left alone together, Kathy would implore Walter with constant murmurings not to intervene, even though he was so inclined, and that despite his own helpless, timid spirit. Instead, he lay curled up in his unobtrusive corner, watching the travesties unfold; saddened beyond belief.

Helplessly, he watched the reenactments of his recollections now, while the apparition of the girl moved about the room cautiously intense, engaged deeply in her cleaning chores, and wary of the man's always imminent return. That most lucid memory, however, could not quite allow the monster to come back into the room – not yet. Walter wanted to savor the precious moment when he and the little girl had the old place effectively to themselves, as if they were the sole inhabitants of their – by necessity - make-believe, made-up world. Walter also sensed the apparition of the mother as she lay sick within her bed upstairs, herself a victim of the father in this completely isolated house so far out in the woods, but upstairs was a place – a badder place he sensed – where he would not ever choose to venture.

Periodically, the girl would pause within the details of her work and take a moment to pay her Walter some much-desired and appreciated attention, alert as always for the sound outside that would mark the man's return. Since Walter could smell the father's smell, even as it entered stealthily into the back yard, he always let the girl - with a tiny little whimper - know that the paternal demon had, unfortunately, come back.

He made that same sound now as the apparition of the father – as if summoned on command - suddenly jerked open, with a squeal of whining hinges, the back door of that old place. Standing silhouetted against the dismissive light outside, dim and gray, he stood just as he had stood back then, surveying the constricted space with laser eyes to pick out the one picayune thing left undone – or done wrong – that would permit him to fly so far off the handle he would hold no obligation for remaining sane. That he needed an excuse – or permission – to indulge himself with such full immersion into his insanity, was an inexplicable adjunct of his bizarre and vile behavior. Once satisfied that he had spotted the thing different from the rest, he was free to boot Walter across the room and approach his little girl with that terrible, imperative, and provocative glint twitching madly from his malevolent eyes, which seemed to glow with the reddish fire of hell whenever he found a proper reason to let go.

And he always did let go on her.

Sometimes – this time – prior to letting go, he would approach her like a stalker, slowly and warily, but with an inevitability that spoke of fiendish, anticipatory needs. And because Kathy had begged him not to intercede, Walter could only watch the demon's back as he hunched over the little girl, cooing to her with his kind of pig-like grunting as he handled her roughly and intrusively – anything but like a father. Until this one time – the one re-enacted by the apparitions of this, his worst memory of all – when Walter heard the girl suddenly squeal out in pain, saw the father flinch, then watched him bring his fist down in a fury of retribution for not remaining utterly quiet and submissively still. The crunch of fist on bone is what finally caused Walter - terrified and angry - to finally overcome his self-imposed passivity and to launch himself ferociously at the man, tearing into his beefy thigh with a vengeance too long held in check, ripping the clothes and flesh away as rabidly as he could, seeking only to displace the man from his grip upon the girl, and hopefully, to make him leave the room. With an inhuman howl of pain, and unable to dislodge the inflamed beast from his agonized and screaming leg, the man shoved and kicked and flailed his way blindly out the back door, where Walter let him go.

His concern was only for the girl.

When he nuzzled solicitously up to her hunched over little form, he knew immediately that she had been hurt quite badly. He wanted to lick her desperate face, but it was already swollen, turning a splotched and yellowish purple brown, and she was bleeding profusely from her crooked little nose – so newly broken. What happened next came to Walter instinctively, for he sensed the man would be gone only long enough to bring back with him disaster and final retribution in the form of some lethal weapon. So he nudged and prodded and finally bit and pulled the little girl's dress – the same one she had wrapped him in when saving him from the woods – and led her numb and disoriented little body out the door, across the desolated yard, and into the narrow rutted road that passed by the wretchedness that was the signature of the old place.

Walter could not have known that fate had decided to intervene in favor of the little girl, but perhaps he sensed that too, for he had not led her that far down the road when he heard and then saw the car approaching – a rare and unusual occurrence on this outback road, where visitors never came, and travelers had no need. Kathy and Walter stood waiting quietly, watching apprehensively for the car to come near, and when it did, it stopped. A man was driving; a woman sat beside him, and it was she who opened up the door, looked long and hard at Kathy - with Walter poised protectively at her side - and spoke quietly and low.

"Who did this to you?" she asked, a tremor in her voice.

Not obviously aware of her immediate surroundings, or the meaning of the car, the man, or the lady, and maybe not even of the question she had been asked, Kathy answered with the truth, for it was the only thing she knew for sure.

"My daddy," she replied. And then, as if to clarify, "My daddy hit me."

"You poor child," the woman responded, her maternal pride as wounded as the small bedraggled girl standing so dejectedly before her. "You get yourself in this car right now. You're going with us for a ride."

And when the little girl hesitated - for her father had brainwashed her well and true about the way to handle strangers - Walter nudged her from behind, and did so forcibly until she had been pushed right up to the woman, who took her in her arms – clucking in sympathy all the while – lifted her up into the car, and then, looking warily around, aware of what a father's wrath might entail, she gingerly deposited her into the back seat of the car, turned to Walter and said, "Not you," and told the man to drive. Walter was left alone to watch them go. From the back window, the little girl's face – damaged in so many ways – watched him for a long and final time.

Walter sat there by the road long after the car had disappeared.

He had nothing else to do but sit, to begin remembering forever the fevered and abandoned look upon the little girl's face, the look that said so many things: like thank you and I'll miss you and I wish that you could come with me too and I wish I knew what is going to happen to me next and I wonder if I shall ever see you – my dearest friend - again.

Walter's face must have looked the same.

He felt the sharp and burning pain before he heard the shot.

And he knew that he was dead.

Sitting curled up in the corner of the old place now, Walter still waited patiently, and as he waited, he remembered somewhat vaguer memories. He had wandered for so long amongst the woods and shadows of another world, a world of somewhere just to be, a darker world without the little girl, but a world where he had been allowed to wander far and wide, and always far away from this place to which he had only now – reluctantly - returned. He had not known love again, or experienced the wonderful attention of one beloved friend, or even known the presence of inattentive people, or others of his kind. He had known only isolation and dark forebodings, and an inability to leave this world, for he could never leave without knowing what had happened to the girl – his precious, damaged little girl. And he had always stayed far away from the old place – and the demon that had become a man - until now.

Because, he had heard her call at last, and he could not ignore such unbridled need.

The apparitions of his past faded themselves away, having served the purpose of his recollections, leaving the old place truly empty and deserted, and Walter felt again the loneliness that had tortured him for so long. He had never been allowed the grace to know what happened to the little girl: if she had found refuge from her father; if she had grown beautiful and strong; if she had known happiness and love; if she remembered him at all.

Now he waited to find out.

When he felt a warm and loving presence at the door, Walter knew that she had come to him at last. He rose slowly to his feet and watched the door begin to slowly open. And standing on the threshold, he saw the gleaming beauty of a woman who was radiated through and through by an incredibly bright light shining forth from both her body and her face – even though she seemed quite old, with hair as white as snow, and a face wrinkled from a life perhaps long and hard, although her smile suggested memories filled mostly with overwhelming kindness and some necessary happiness – and as he watched, the woman transformed before him, like some transcendent wraith, into the little girl lodged forever within the woman, and she was smiling at him too. And with a shining, tearful happiness at seeing Walter once again, she softly spoke to him the words he had waited so desperately to hear.

"I have come for you," she said, dropping to her knees and embracing her old friend with a wondrous mixture of sadness and relief. "You have wandered much too long, my friend. You have been too long alone."

And then she told him of her life. She answered the questions he had held while sitting by the road, watching her looking back at him from the window, disappearing from his view, just before he had been shot.

"I loved you so much," she said. "You were my hero. You saved my life. I was so sad for you, not knowing what became of the poor abandoned whelp I found shivering in the woods. I did not know until recently – until my own demise - what happened to you that day, nor how you wandered all alone in darkness afterward, not knowing what became of me. How you could not move on because of your concern. But Walter, my whole world changed because of you and what you did. My life with those people who found us on the road was mostly good. They made of me their own, and I was young and quite resilient, and my horrid childhood in the old place – this old place – at some point became just a barely recalled nightmare to my newer dreams, bright and lovely dreams that brought so many better things for me. My only sadness left was all for you – so utterly left behind and all alone. Left behind with...him. And now I know, I was quite right to be so sad for you. I could not know your fate, and I wish with all my heart that you could have come with me on that day. I wish you could have been a part of my new life. I wish I could have loved you then forever.

I wish I had known that afterward you wandered.

I wish I could have helped you to move on.

She paused then, took Walter's face gently into her hands, and looked deeply into his mournful but contented eyes.

"But now I can," she said.

"Walter, it is now the time for us to be moving on. It is time for you to stop your endless wandering and painful remembering. It is time for you to come with me at last. You and me, my dear, we are going on a journey into light.

"My hero, my old friend, the darkness is done with you."

Walter whimpered at the happiness embedded in her words.

And he realized then what had always been her most unbridled need.

Her need had always been for him.

THE END

BY DEMONS POSSESSED

*B*ack in the beginning, before their worlds merged, the demons thought that humanoids were sheep: docile and not prone to partaking in their ghastly, nasty revelries. And this was fine with them, as they found great satisfaction by indulging in their more profane proclivities solely amongst themselves. The humans thought of them as just a darker side of nature, and were not inclined toward further investigations, although they did take minor steps to ward off any stray intrusions from such evil inclinations. They made dolls and such, on which they performed oddly superstitious rites. And they warned the children. But in the beginning, separate is how things were...and how they remained for quite a while.

An odd characteristic of evil, however, and perhaps of good as well, is that eventually it gets bored with the whole status quo of diddling solely with itself, and eventually – always - it seeks for more. Greed and evil – and perhaps good – are joined securely at the hip. It is just that the greediness of evil seems somehow more profound, for while hope may reign eternal, nullifying somewhat the joy of doing good forever, evil is like an ever-seeking, ever-pining, entropic force, searching out new worlds of joy and happiness and hope for the sole and final purpose of their ultimate destruction - to leave behind them only a dark and meaningless abyss. For them, the proponents of evil, this is glee. And though the humans were not particularly beings possessed by overwhelming joy and happiness, they would suffice unto the moment.

The first time that a demon possessed a human, it was a uniquely new occurrence and experience, as defining and presumptive for future generations as each particular moment written down in Genesis, for it set the method and the approach, the mental articulation, and the physical and psychological culmination for all times yet to come. Not to mention any future symbolism and iconic replications adapted later for popular ritualization by all of the yet-to-be descendants – both humanoid and demonic – birthed upon on the heels of that initial possessive act. These ritualizations, it must be said, also became impregnated by the former rituals of religion, and thereafter became an integral part and parcel of the ceremonial spiritual re-enactments based upon the original worshippings themselves.

As if the demons had been with them...forever.

It behooves one then, to bear witness to the defining moment as it initially and actually occurred.

The demon who was chosen by the unrelenting willfulness of an intrinsically immoral force, and acting on his own inability to contain within himself the inordinately expansive growth that such a volcanic and explosive force entailed, was not the woman Lilith, that so-called original demon canonized and institutionalized by later Middle Ages folk, for Lilith was first of all a human, and only later was she reportedly made into a demon by the great Lucifer himself. The details are rather sketchy on how that allegedly was accomplished, probably because that is not the truth of how it happened. In fact, the demonology of the Church is not the subject here, and no matter how demonic-acting the first women may have been, they were not – in and of themselves – actual demons... at least, not at that time.

The actual demons were born – or created, or made, or conjured – first.

One of them - the one predestined to endure the un-ignorable, and perhaps ignoble, arising into critical mass of that irresistible immoral need so eloquently described above, a situation actually experienced as demonic boredom, or existential dissatisfaction – had acquired by universal agreement, or simply a twisted quirk of fate, the name of *Basil*. And in a strangely perverted misuse of theological annotation, *Basil* was: *the chosen one*. He did not have to think about this much; he simply rose up from his place before the fire – demons rather worshipped fire – and followed his sniffing, predatory nose to where the humans gathered.

He was looking for a woman.

Actually, he went sniffing for a woman, which is how it's really done.

*****

The woman sat apart from most of the others in her community. It was that time of month for her for which both the women and the men had already conjured up a plethora of euphemistic phrases and allusions, but mostly it was the time to best be left alone. She did not feel ostracized or alienated; she actually felt respected and even somewhat exclusively important, as if the others recognized how she could best be served by spending meditative time in seclusion with herself. She tended to her own individual fire, though she remained within easy sight of the others' rather larger blaze, and though she kept company with only her own thoughts, still she could hear the murmuring conversation of the community at large as they mingled around that larger, more inclusive blaze.

So, she was not entirely alone.

Her name was Rebecca Mae.

She was not chilled by the lateness of the evening - her little fire kept her warm – but she felt a foreign chill nonetheless, as if something in the night had taken form and run its bony finger down her spine. She shivered in response. And she noticed that her thoughts had come to quite a sudden standstill; that she suddenly felt intensely wary, as if a predatory beast were waiting patiently just beyond the firelight to pounce upon her solitary self and carry her off screaming into the woods. She almost forgot to breathe, as did the very air around her – now sitting just as still as her own unwavering, brittle thoughts.

It was as if the night had *shushed* itself.

And now - worse than any chilling, prevailing sense of horror from some nocturnal prowling beast about to strike her dead – came a sense of infernal, horrid laughter, an evil chuckling that crept up close and personal right beside her ear, and for this she knew that she would scream. Except, a crusty hand had already clamped itself to her mouth, as a fetid odor wafted up her nose, and she could neither inhale her own necessary gasp of breath to scream, nor let it rip itself from her thoroughly scalded throat. She could only endure the nasty smell of terror and succumb to the paralyzing fear that it provoked, waiting endlessly to feel the fatal, spine-snapping bite that would surely plunge itself deep into her neck.

The fatal bite, however, did not come.

Instead, a liquid presence began to ooze itself into her very soul, making her feel like she had immersed herself in a lake of heated oil. A very strange and weird immediate effect upon her mental state and observations made her now look upon the community sitting rather gaily around the larger blaze – her family and her friends – as obsequious, ingratiating irritants to her separate being; enemies to the core. The children, most especially, appeared to her abusively manipulated senses as particularly vile and odious creatures, things to be abhorred, and yes, perhaps were necessarily subject now to immediate annihilation, and so she stood up from her paltry fire, with another blazing hotly from her eyes, and she began walking toward the larger flames with total conflagration on her mind.

And what she felt was glee.

*****

Basil was ecstatic with that which he had wrought.

The charred remains of all the humans that encircled the blazing fire stirred his innermost being with such a burst of insane delight that he could hardly bear the intensity of his gladness. But what stirred him even more was the unforgiveable disgust that had blossomed deep inside the soul of Rebecca Mae, a most unexpected and delicious surprise that he could feed upon like a ravenous, scavenging beast; savoring each saturated morsel as if it were a blood-engorged, still-warm major organ ripped from within her bosom – just like any rabid wolf would tear the still-beating heart from a mortally wounded hare.

It made him salivate - uncontrollably.

It made him do a wicked little dance; a perverted little jig.

It made him quiver with the prospect of a twisted, sexual delight.

And just like that, the demons became addicted to the human race. They fed upon their soulful disgust like routing pigs trapped inside a waste-impregnated trough; then they fed upon their insipient dread like supplicants at communion; and finally, they began to savor their sensuously raw anticipation like an appetizer before an erotically orgasmic feast. And though the humans finally began to suspect that their anticipatory dread itself was what called the demons to them, like a bee might find its way to honey, or like a rasty dog to a bitch suffused with heat, they simply could not eliminate the causatory factor of such expectant fear, nor purge the poisonous, titillating pulsing of their own fully quickened blood as it flowed inexorably toward an inevitably disastrous destiny in their spidery, networked veins. In time, they too began to feel a sense of glee, as they – like any child with a proclivity for trouble – sensed a possible, if wicked, delight in the opportunity for individual possession.

Ironically, this transformation in the humans - which made them seem almost welcoming of the resulting devastation from such a parasitic and demonic personal invasion – served to dissuade the demons for a while from pursuing their more vile incubations. For, their satisfaction came as much from the human's utter revulsion at the penetrating act as it did from the ultimate disruption of any joy and happiness therein contained, not to mention the chaotic violence which often ensued and was executed as a necessary result upon the larger community all around. The massacred remains of ever-growing numbers of dead and rotting bodies, usually twisted into ghastly-figured shapes due to the supremely venal nature of the violence committed, made a lovely sacred ground for all the demons, who often wandered aimlessly around the perimeters of such a massive death-ground, drinking in the ambience of terror that had preceded the awful slaughter, mitigating any disappointment they may have felt towards the humans' almost willful submission to their gruesome, fatal end.

The demons had to accept the fact that the humans were always on the lookout for them now; trying to predict which fated one among their number would be the next to fall, and who would then spread a kind of epic havoc amongst the rest. And though they pretended to be repulsed, their hypocrisy was brightly evident to the demons, who accommodated rapidly to the fact that the humans were simple, easy-going sheep no more, but merely ravenous partakers in their own self-created carnage, themselves clothed in but a modicum of falsifying camouflage; in other words: wolves in sheep's clothing.

And thus, at last, the worlds of the demons and the humans began to truly merge. Which marked the middle ages of their being; a time to up the level of their game; a necessity arising for the demons to become much more adept at denigrating the society of humans.

For this, they turned to God.

*****

The priest was genuine.

The real deal.

Le Révérend Père Guillaume - or William, or just Father Bill – was known by his French parishioners to be a humble but holy man of God. He was an excellent, shepherding man of the cloth, tending to his flock with all the conscientiousness that he exhibited while doting upon his sacred little rectory garden – the one beloved by the children - which he did daily and religiously, often bringing to his corporate mission the same diligence and skills he used while puttzing about his small but impressively immaculate and well-kept *jardin,* using both cunning and anointing to weed-out the ne'er-do-wells who sometimes threatened to disrupt the holiness of his carefully selected and guided protectees. He was particularly and acutely attuned to unmasking any errant and misguided wolf in sheep's clothing who should wander – either by ill-intent, or simply unfortunate misdirection – into their midst. Once revealed by Father Bill's two-edged *sword of truth,* the culprit was duly and expeditiously sent upon his way.

Unusual, then, when Father Bill entertained the demon in his own garden.

He did not know it was a demon, for the one known as Damian had already possessed the unwary, swarthy human source whom he used to infiltrate the rectory yard and whisper so insidiously into Father William's left and less discriminating ear. The priest was mostly oblivious to the fact that someone knelt just behind him as he gardened – himself crouched down upon his knees – or that the mostly non-existent person had his mouth so near to touching the good Father's non-discriminating ear that he should have been mightily discomfited, but he was not. In fact, he was intrigued. For the demons had learned from their mergence with the humans not to be so dramatic as when

Basil had beguiled Rebecca Mae by clasping himself tightly to her throat. Their methods now were much more subtle, and therefore increasingly salacious, like with Damian well-ensconced inside the human and whispering with the smoothness of a slithering snake into the waiting – almost inviting – wide-open ear of the self-involved and much too self-preoccupied priest.

What Damian whispered to Father Bill is of little or no concern.

How the priest reacted – when the children began walking by - is.

But how the demon reacted was even worse: supremely orgasmic in his delight. And not because the damage to the children was so severe, but precisely because of how the priestly soul reacted to its own – completely unforeseen – degredation and ungodly succubation. It was this revulsion that most captivated Damian and left him drooling at the dissolutionary distress of Father Bill. He was almost disappointed when the good and humble, godly priest put an ultimate and untimely end to his unendurable and unforgivable suffering, and went to meet, if not his God, at least the arbiter of his eternal fate.

And Damian immediately went off to find another man of God.

While the other demons continued to evolve.

*****

Thus we come to modern times, when demons and humans have become effectively inseparable by nature. No more clenchings of unprotected throats; no more whisperings into unwary ears. No more reluctant entertainings, or invitations to temptation. Just apparent humans filled with demonic inclinations roaming at will along the city sidewalks and driving down city streets. And sometimes walking into schools, fully armed

Or possibly, even worse.

Like Donald Robert – human/demon extraordinaire. Just an everyday Joe, corrupted by his ancestral genes, at large amongst the denizens of the second largest city in the world – and thus, invisible to the masses. On the prowl for something to whet his appetite, and upon which to gorge his culinary senses for the macabre; something with which to satisfy those insatiable demonic inclinations given birth - or created, or made, or conjured – so very long ago; nurtured and sadistically developed and finessed over such a long span of human-measured time that the predator no longer wears the clothing of his prey.

The sheep has now become the wolf – ravenous with hunger.

And D.R. is very hungry.

Demons no longer prey upon the helpless, nor do they seek out the inordinately good – those were simply and ultimately but single, faltering, necessary steps upon the particularly long and ever-learning path they were forced to follow – manifesting their evil all the way - in order to get them inexorably to the here and now: where the humans they seek out for immoral satisfaction are, in actual fact, the ones most like themselves. In the end, you see, their motivation is purely self-destructive.

Donald Robert – like the demoralized human that he inhabits – is sniffing out another human who most exemplifies his deconstructed self, even though in this case, perhaps ironically, the human is a woman. Of course, the woman is as yet uninhabited herself; therein lies the fun. And Donald Robert understands a delicious fact learned first with Father Bill, when demon lust was suddenly discovered to be accentuated most when prompted by the humans' acquiescence and invitation – an active willingness on the humans' part to entertain the notion of wildly errant thoughts, and then to take action on the insidious whisperings inside their heads. There is nothing quite so exquisite to the demons as when an uninhabited human surrenders willingly to their lead. The moment is supremely, agonizingly pre-climactic, and so close to the consequently orgasmic release of death as to send the demonic presence into paroxysms of lethal, frenzied fury.

D.R. is quivering in anticipative splendor.

Because, oh yes, he smells her now.

Following her enticing scent, he walks the city sidewalks as aggressively as any dog obsessed by the aroma of his latest bitch's heat, head down, following a trail that only he can see, turning corners without thinking, crossing streets only by identification with other preoccupied pedestrians – the ones who somehow sense when all the others are just about to step off the sidewalk curb – then matching their quickened gaits stride for gallant stride across the busy road, until he comes abruptly to the gigantic park and stops, his nostrils quivering with the proximity of his prey.

She is sitting quietly alone upon a bench, reading.

Waiting.

The demon in D.R. can smell her loneliness, recently acquired.

So too he smells the hurt; the desperation; the need for isolation – the need to be alone. And most of all, he smells the incomparable need she has to heal.

And Donald Robert smiles.

No meek and mild sheep's clothing adorns his body. He is transparently outfitted now as most obviously the wolf, his suit immaculately tailored, his hair professionally groomed, his eyes as cold as steel, and his heart long ago caged in steel. These were all the things that once were only thoughts – errant thoughts whispered into his brain - telling him the kind of man that he might be, if only....if.

He slinks up to the woman.

Waiting for the moment.

When he will say something beguiling to her.

And she will smile.

*****

The demons have been with us forever.
Now...we are them.

THE END

THE DEAD DUMMY

*W*hen Clarence died, Wallace tried to keep the act alive.
After all, they had talked about this beforehand. But then, they had always talked - about so many things. It seemed as if their every moment was spent talking, with rarely a silent moment wasted between them. They were partners, and they had been partners since the moment Clarence suddenly appeared in Wallace's humdrum, mundane life. They took to each other immediately; Clarence fortuitously adding the spark of a somewhat sardonic, somewhat sarcastic, always spirited humor to the intensely serious musings of Wallace, who was completely befuddled and bewildered by the world at large. And probably that is what drew Wallace to Clarence's attention in the first place. As for Wallace: well, he just loved the dummy at first sight. He could not have said exactly why, although that bizarrely over-sized head – larger than Wallace's own – certainly garnered his early fascination. Admittedly, Clarence was exceptionally ugly – suffering both from acute rosacea as well as ultra-thinning hair - a determination readily authenticated by the reactions of those who saw him hanging listlessly from the shop's ceiling; sometimes accompanied by little shrieks of muffled horror when they noticed his unblinking, staring eyes – outbursts which Clarence tended to ignore, but which Wallace never could bring himself to quite forgive.

When Wallace brought him home, the two of them made a deal. Clarence was not opposed to playing the buffoon - after all, he was just the dummy – but he would not dumb down his humor only to make the ventriloquist look good. In return, with Wallace as the straight man, pretending to make his dummy talk, Clarence promised not to make the man look stupid, just perhaps naïve, in that good-natured, heartwarming sort of way that made the ladies smile; that made them want to – oh so much – help that poor, pathetic man. Wallace instantly agreed. They never really had to plan their act, because the repartee between them came naturally and fast, primarily due to Clarence's piercing humor and Wallace's gullible naïveté. After all, Wallace never had to program Clarence's words, and he never had to really speak for him. He just pretended with his always slightly moving lips.

Clarence did the rest.

At home, they talked much more seriously about the ills and woes that plagued the world, things they mocked while performing on the stage, where they were seeking laughter more than money. They were not so sanguine about such topics when sitting in their small, two-man apartment, usually at the rickety kitchen table on their rickety wooden chairs, sharing perhaps a pot of unusually thick and potent coffee, and just perhaps, each with a dollop of brandy hidden in his cup. Clarence might still be sardonic and sarcastic, but never did he belittle the sincerity with which Wallace bemoaned the current, dilapidated condition of the world and the state of its immorality, for the dummy knew how much that Wallace missed the insanely magical world of his youth, and he felt a great compassion for the disillusioned and desperate child become a man.

"Wally, I know just what you mean," Clarence would often say. "I, too, miss the wonders of my youth. And you can just imagine the obstacles in my way. You know, the head and all. Hanging around in stores. Rarely spoken to. Certainly never asked to join in childhood games. Always the observer. But, we never really know what might come next. After all, you did walk into the store that day."

And Wallace smiled at the memory.

Clarence always knew how to make him smile and feel better about the world, if only for the moment.

"That was quite the day," admitted Wallace. "You, up there, staring down, with that half-crazed look. Your tiny pupils merely pinpoints within their whites. Looking at me as if you expected me to say 'hello'. Which, as I recall, I did. Not expecting you to answer, but then you did, and I don't think I've ever been as happy as I was the moment when you spoke."

"Nor I," said Clarence, looking totally sincere due to his unblinking eyes.

They liked to reminisce like that, recalling especially the earliest days together, when everything seemed so fresh and new.

On stage, they would often banter back and forth:

Wallace: *So, my friend, what brings you out here on this fine day?*

Clarence (looking at him strangely): *Uh, that would be your hand?*

(Pause.)

Clarence: *Which, by the way, is rather poorly placed, if I might say. Would you care to shift it just a bit?*

(Pause.)

Clarence: *Oh, that felt rather nice. Might you do that once again?*

(Audience laughter.)

(Wallace looks chagrined.)

They made a lot of fun about their unique physical arrangement, creating uneasiness and discomfort - but also laughter - in those who had gathered 'round to watch their act. Because Clarence always had a slightly conspiratorial smile plastered to his face, and because Wallace always had a slightly pained expression upon his – due, of course, to the need for keeping his lips apparently sealed while Clarence spoke – the audience was always left to wonder about the inherent intimacy between the dummy and the man; just another tailored reason for the compassionate ladies in the group to want – oh so much – to help.

As for the world at large, the two were ruthless in their observations and condemnations, both on the stage and not, and this too made the crowds self-consciously but pleasantly uncomfortable, and yet amused and entertained as well. The dummy and the man had ways of saying things that the people had always felt were true, but were too constrained by society to admit. Laughter became the conspiratorial method by which they offered up their hidden but heartfelt strong agreements.

And they could not help but laugh at this obnoxious pair, or even at themselves when so addressed.

Wallace: *So, my friend, what do you think of our new President?*

Clarence: *That jackass with the beastly ugly wife?*

(Audience gasps.)

Wallace: *Now, now, he is the duly elected leader of our country.*

Clarence: *Well, any partner that ugly deserves a hand up her ....*

Wallace (interrupting quickly): *Whoa, my friend...that's the First Lady we're talking about!*

Clarence: *Yeah the first lady ever to have a hand up her ....*

Wallace: *Stop now! You're being quite insulting!*

(Clarence turns his head to stare at Wallace.)

Clarence: *Not as insulting as the President's hand, I bet.*

(Again the audience gasps.)

Wallace: *I really don't understand how you can say such things.*

(Clarence looks incredulous.)

Clarence: *Well, they're your lips moving, bubba. I can see them.*

(Wallace stops talking. So does Clarence. They stare each other down.)

(The audience laughs.)

Clarence (turning his head away and murmuring): *Fine way to talk about the jackass and his jenny.*

(The First Lady happens to share this moniker for a female ass.)

(The audience pauses, gasps again, then cannot help but indulge their guilty laughter.)

And on it goes.

At home, they might discuss the same events, but Clarence – in consideration of his friend – was not so boldly humorous. And this was not all they talked about, for they were indeed friends, so they talked about the inner, secret things that each man had carried within himself for years. Although one might think that Clarence would carry more demons inside than Wallace - him being the one to endure the many hurtful jeers and taunts about his size, his head, his ugliness, and those unendurable, piercing little eyes – actually it was Wallace who had suffered more, perhaps because he tended to absorb and cling tenaciously to the seemingly endless disappointments of the world – the diminishing amount of magic, as it were. Clarence offered in return his own harder won empathy and compassion.
And maybe, just a bit of magic, too.
So, it came as a surprise one day, as Wallace had been going on rather eloquently about his dismal perceptions of the world, when Clarence seemed inattentive and unresponsive to his complaints. The dummy sat there, and even with the false attention registered within his non-blinking eyes, there seemed to be no spark inside them, and certainly no sympathetic understanding, but just a kind of listless inattention, or mindless preoccupation. Wallace's ongoing elucidations came to an abruptly interrupted end as he studied his old friend, and then he began to worry.

"Clarence?" he prodded.

Which garnered him no immediate response.

"Clarence?" he repeated, poking the dummy with a finger.

"Huh?" Clarence finally responded, in a way most uncharacteristic of him; in a way, as if he truly were a dummy.

"What's wrong?"

"What?"

"You're acting strange. You, know, for you," said Wallace, trying to add a bit of humor, which was not his strong suit.

"I'm not feeling well."

"You're not..."

But Wallace was too taken aback by these words to finish his own sentence. Not once in the history of their partnership had Clarence ever expressed anything remotely related to his own physical well-being. That alone should have worried Wallace. But he could swear his old friend's eyes were drooping, and that worried him even more.

"My god, man, what is wrong with you?"

"I think I'm sick," came the strained response.

"Sick!" Wallace exclaimed, as if incapable of registering the meaning of that remark. "How in the world can you be sick?"

"I don't know," the dummy responded, sounding like he might cry.

And then he added, "Really sick. This is not good."

With just those few incredibly implausible words, a final magic began to wind its way out of Wallace's supremely well-manicured personal world. For a realization hit him then, one which obliterated his well-structured edifice of personal comfort and personal understanding: he could not take Clarence to a doctor. Not only were there no doctors practicing for dummies, he would himself be declared institutionally insane – clinically and professionally – if he were to take him to any normal doctor for proper treatment.

Wallace began to panic.

And Clarence noticed.

"I'm so sorry," he uttered. "But something is very wrong with me."

"It's okay," Wallace said, recovering quickly within this newly arisen emergency. "We'll do something. We'll make it better."

"How?'

"I don't know."

But as Clarence lapsed into a kind of somnolescent state, Wallace tried to think harder than he had ever thought before. He had no idea how to treat the dummy, mostly because he had no idea what could be wrong with him. The fact that Clarence was feeling ill made no sense to him whatsoever. He had just assumed that his friend was immune to all human-centric ills, including any serious disease that might wander across his path. Wallace had to discount that presumption now, as obviously something quite extraordinary was happening to his partner – his lifetime friend. And no matter how much thinking that he applied, Wallace discovered that he could do absolutely nothing that would help.

The two men eventually accommodated to this heartsick situation, slowly coming to the realization there was nothing to be done but to simply watch and wait.

And talk.

"What do you suppose might be waiting for me over there?" Clarence asked his friend one day.

It might have been a somewhat idle question, something a dummy might muse upon like a normal person would idly explore a piece of candy in his mouth, but Wallace suspected a deeper motive behind the question, and in his nervousness he once again attempted humor.

"A dummy paradise, maybe? A bunch of dummy virgins?"

If Clarence had been able, he would have rolled his eyes. But noticing his unamused demeanor, Wallace tried again.

"I don't know, Bud. What might any of us expect to find waiting for us there?"

"You know what I mean, Wally. What is someone like me supposed to expect? Do you believe in wooden souls? Shall I ride a rocking horse to heaven?"

Wallace was not comfortable with this at all.

"There must be something for you there," he said. "Something grand, I hope."

But he himself was not convinced.

Clarence was considerate enough to let the question lie, and it occurred to him at that moment that he would need to be the one to see his old friend through this – he would need to be the strong one. Wallace had endured too much taken from his youth for him to deal with this now – too much magic gone; just disappeared. And that is why Clarence approached him later with his plan, one he hoped would make his leaving bearable for Wallace; perhaps giving him hope to carry on. Thus it was, while sitting once again around the kitchen table, on their wooden kitchen chairs, drinking their strong, brandy-laced coffee, that Clarence the dummy made the following bemusing suggestion.

"Why don't you just go ahead and carry on with our act," he said.

"What?" Wallace was indeed bemused.

"Think about it, Wally. I mean, what's to stop you? It's not like anyone would know that I was gone. What, my eyes don't even move? No shit, like that's something new. You can still make my mouth move up and down with that irritating string I've got in back. The only difference is, you'll have to do the talking now. Pretend that I am speaking."

"But..."

"But what, Wally? You're just gonna have to do the ventriloquism thing for real now. That's all. Why, it'd be just like old times!"

"But you won't be there," Wallace protested.

"Like I said, who'd know?"

Wallace knew precisely who would know, but Clarence seemed suddenly so exuberantly optimistic and genuinely happy that he could not bear to burst his momentary bubble. And that is how he came to agree about carrying on with their act.

He would do it for his friend.

Still, things did not go well.

Maybe it was because he was coming off an extended period of debilitating grief and had not yet relearned to cope. For even if Clarence were still present physically – obviously, he was not prone to biological decay – and though his eyes, as forestated, remained steadfastly open, it was more than obvious that no light bulb burned inside: there was nobody home. And this distressed poor Wallace beyond belief. The ways he chose to cope with his grief were quite bizarre: often placing the dead dummy at the kitchen table as if he were still inclined to talk, even placing a steaming hot cup of brandied coffee before him and warning him not to drink; pretending to still confide in his old and dearest friend the things that bugged him most about the world. Still, even in his wildest imagination, the dummy did not answer.

Wallace sank deeply into depression.

It is hard to say how much time passed him by like this. Suffice it to mention, a day did come when he remembered their earlier conversation, and the recollection was like a prod to his self-esteem and dignity, telling him to buck himself up, grab his dead dummy, and hit the road.

And so he did.

The first time he appeared on stage like this, he almost convinced himself that he could pull it off. After all, Clarence sat there like the dummy that he really was - eyes propped wide open; that supercilious smirk plastered to his face - and when Wallace manipulated the string that moved his mouth, twisted his head so that he appeared to be reacting, and pretended to be speaking in Clarence's distinctive manner – sardonic and sarcastic – he really thought he might convince the audience that all was well.

Except...he could not advance the repartee between the dummy and himself, because he had no way to know what witty remarks Clarence would spontaneously produce in response to his own obscenely mundane provocations. And thus, their dialogue sounded like the echoing refrains of a rather simple-minded man simply talking to himself.

Wallace: *So, what do you think of the President?*

Clarence: *That donkey? The one with the wife?*

(Audience is deathly quiet)

Wallace: *Now, now, he's the leader of our country.*

Clarence: *Well, his hand is where it shouldn't be.*

Wallace: *Whoa, that's the First Lady we're talking about!*

Clarence: *Yeah the first lady with his hand up her butt.*

(Now the audience gasps.)

Wallace: *Stop now! You're just being insulting!*

(Clarence turns his head to look emptily at Wallace)

Clarence: *Not as insulting as your hand.*

(The audience begins to murmur and shuffle in their spots.)

Wallace: *How can you say such things?*

(Clarence looks dumbfounded)

Clarence: *Cuz you're talking.*

(Wallace stops talking. So does Clarence. They stare each other down.)

(The audience begins to grimace.)

Clarence (turning his head away and murmuring): *Fine. Let's talk about something else.*

And on it goes.

Wallace did not really understand the problem. He never fully understood the amazingly exuberant laughter, uncomfortable as it might be, that Clarence had always been able to elicit from the crowds. He never understood to what extent exactly that he had been the butt of his own brilliant dummy's jokes, as harmless and benign as Clarence intended them to be, and he certainly never understood the humor to be found within those serious complaints that he himself had consistently expressed about the world.
    What Wallace now understood clearly and completely was that Clarence had been the act.
    And that Clarence was truly gone.
    That the magic had entirely left his world.
    That he was truly on his own.
    And so, what happened next should have been no surprise.

*****

The team of Clarence and Walter only appeared on stage one final time. Wallace felt that he had let his partner down, and he was determined to give it another go. Perhaps that initial return performance had been premature and too poorly planned for proper execution. Prior to their final stint, Wallace spent his time remembering the precise elocutions of Clarence during their most-applauded acts, and he was positive he could replicate the memory by refusing to improvise on the spot. By the time they took their customary spots, with Wallace – dressed to the nines in his contemporary new black suit – sitting on the upright cushioned chair, with Clarence perched clumsily but securely on his lap, Wallace was feeling mightily confident, and even feeling as if the spirit of the poor departed dummy might actually be present.

Alas, his intuition proved to be spot on.

For when he asked his dummy the first question of the day, before he could manipulate the string, before he could throw his other voice, a disembodied speaking - croaking so obviously from the grave that the little children cried – gave forth the following horrid utterance:

"Greetings from the other side, you sniveling, ignorant oaf."

THE END

THE WATCHING MAN

The watching man is back.
Every twelve years, like clockwork, he returns.
I had to reconstruct his deeply pernicious schedule after my earliest memories were triggered by subsequent events, but his first appearance in my life logged in precisely - as suspected - at twelve years old. So that is the recollection that I will first relate, although his connection to the direst events occurring throughout my life did not dawn on me until much later, and that is of course what most concerns me now at the fragile age of eighty-four.

When I was but twelve years old, I had experienced enough of life to know that not everything goes your way. Not only that, but I had even accommodated to the fact – a little, anyway – that sometimes that might be for the best. I had also known the kind of titillating terror that comes from watching movies based on horror and television shows that provocatively showcase much the same. But I had never known real terror in my life, nor had I yet suspected that movies and TV shows might somehow bleed into the reality of my everyday being, not until that foggy night – the fog was instrumental to my fright – when the watching man first made his appearance in my world.

As one often reads in stories of the weird, I felt his watching on me first, like an uninvited hand upon my shoulder, the kind that is sometimes meant to be consoling but more often is endured as if it were a personal intrusion. Which is how his attention felt to me. It made me turn my head. And when I did, I could not at first decipher my own perception. It was like I saw an oval blackness emerging from the fog – a blackness owning one pair of eyes, a nose, and mouth, but only as depressions in a mask – and the blackness was not human, but shiny like that of the most brilliant, exotic Asian beetle, and I was made to think – even at that young age, a time when science-fiction was only just about to blossom – *that thing must certainly be a robot.*

He stood as still as any robot.

Watching. Just watching.

The street lamp by which he stood made the shining of his glistening skin look ever that much more brilliant, reflecting two round patches atop his shaven head that looked like two pools of extra eyes, and made his normal eyes retract into his face like sunken ships within a leaden sea; made his artificial nose become the arrow of his unwavering attention, and made of his slightly protruding lips the grimace of an unguessable intention. The relaxed but sturdy settledness in his shoulders, with his listlessly dangling arms, bespoke an infinite capacity for patience, which only made me shiver at the decidedly threatening implication inherent in such a thought.

I was twelve years old; I was not subtle about my staring back.

The odd part is: I don't know when I stopped.

Suddenly, I was no longer outside my house staring across the street at some disconcerting apparition - or a robot dressed in black - apparently risen from the fog. I was in my bedroom, sitting on my bed, reading a familiar book that had occupied me for quite a while. I remember being startled and looking up, but the precise clarity of that earlier scene outside only returned to my complete recollection after having endured similar future visitations. In exactly the same manner, I did not connect the first major tragedy of my life with that visitor's dark appearance; at least, not then. Sitting there on my bed, I wasn't even sure that I had not entirely imagined the watching man. Perhaps I had dozed off for just a bit and he was but a fluff of dissonant association with the book that I was reading. In any case, the next happening in my life thoroughly swept aside all further thought about the eerily appearing, robotic man.

I know you will think that I exaggerate, but my little sister was an answer to a secret prayer that I had prayed for when I was six. I had seen a movie on TV where just such a little girl had adored and become a boon companion to a boy who was very much like me – a little intimidated by the world; a lot confused by the things he saw around him every day; someone who had a bleeding need for total adoration from one who thought he was a hero, a conqueror of foes. Her white knight upon a stallion. That is who I wanted most to be: the hero for a damsel in distress. And, right on cue, my sister came into the world very much attired in distress.

She needed me.

She needed me to carry her around, and later, to push her wheelchair about; to wheel her to the park where she could feel the sun and wind upon her face, could watch the trees dancing to the unseen music embedded in the skies, could listen to the laughter of the children and watch the pigeons feed, and every now and then could find something meant especially for her and me to laugh or cry about. I was twelve years old and she was five, but she did not manage to reach the age I was when first I prayed to have her come into my life. I do not remember how subsequently I came to be thirteen, and yet – unendurably - I did.

Somehow, my life had proceeded on without her.

I was twenty-four when next I saw the watching man, and although I did not remember him from before – not right then – I did feel a chill run through my bones that felt an awful lot like reluctant recollection. I felt the same attention fasten to my neck, the same apprehension grip me unawares, and upon looking across the street from the side on which I walked – this time beneath a brightly sunny sky – I saw a shiny black man posed as still as any statue, and I felt myself cock my head as would a quizzical, befuddled dog, and I knew the kind of recognition that one feels when experiencing déjà vu, not yet realizing that I had indeed known just such a moment once before. I scowled deeply, furrowing my brow, and stared.

Only to awaken deep inside the nearest local coffee shop, huddled over slightly in the non-plush cushioned booth, with my head cradled in my palm and angled to the left, staring out the window at the people passing by. I was cuddled up within a vague but familiar depression, thinking about my sister Lisa as I did most every day, peripherally aware of a dreadful premonition that my day was about to turn itself into something very, very bad.

I'm not sure why I decided to take the alley after leaving the coffee shop that day. I know that after Lisa died I gradually took to avoiding people whenever I could manage, often skirting my way along some shady walls or choosing early morning or later evening to make my way through town. I gravitated toward solitude and seclusion, and the job that I had acquired – making home deliveries of needful drugs to shut-in's and needful supplies to others like myself – allowed me to isolate myself within the tiny cockpit of my car, where, with the right dosage of proper music administered to my ears, I might lose myself in self-immersed delusion. I was not seeking pleasure; I was seeking only my immediate release into oblivion.

The alley was isolated and secluded. Perhaps I gravitated there in the absence of clear thinking. I did not provide an intriguing object for anyone's attention, and likely that is why the running man, after flinging himself from a back door porch, bag in hand, collided so violently into me, knocking both of us to the ground. He was up and gone quite before I noticed his bag idly set beside me, and the people who gathered quickly by my side – the store owner of the slammed-open door was first, of course – all just assumed the bag was mine. And apparently, and awfully coincidentally to my mind, I must have strongly resembled the fleeing man.

In any case, my life as I knew it then was over.

Since I did not spend a full twelve years incarcerated for my guiltless crime, by the time the watching man came into my life again, I was well become a man and getting by completely on my own. I did have trouble getting jobs, but each succeeding job was acquired much more easily, and I gained both credibility and respect as I made my somewhat awkward climb up the heavily-scrutinized corporate ladder. Also, at thirty-six, I knew instantly that the source of gut-wrenching anxiety in my stomach was from seeing the shiny black robotic man standing across the street – watching. By that time, I knew for certain his direct connection to the next really bad thing destined just for me, and though I made a move to cross the street and initiate a darkly desired confrontation, I woke up instead upon a bench, staring emptily into an eerily vacant park.

I knew before I left the park.
I knew that Kathy would not be home when I returned.
I did not know, however, that she would take our dog.
Or that she would also – inexplicably - get me fired.

Now I know what makes a person homeless. For a long time after Kathy left and took the dog and I found myself without a job, I learned about living on the streets, taking meals out of filthy dumpsters, enduring a newfound habit of not showering or cleaning clothes, as well as knowing the mind-numbing but liberating routine of wandering around the city without any clear notion of destination. One quite loses his sense of time as well, and years can pass with no recognition of annual celebrations or anniversaries. Twelve years can pass that way quite easily. At forty-eight, I have no idea what scourge the watching man gifted unto me. Perhaps it was the dirty drugs.

I was clean again at sixty, but getting old. The mind can heal faster and become cleaner than one might at first suppose, considering the wicked damage drugs can do. Due to the nature of the numbers, I passed one whole decade without an encounter with the watching man. But if that gave me cause for hope, the sudden turn of aging into another set of ten – for the first time in this meticulously-episodic-upheaval-pattern to my life – made me pause with anticipation, and this time I began watching for him first. In fact, I pretty much planted myself within a major bus station buried in the city, and I waited.

He did not disappoint for long.

There he was, standing by the station wall, as usual just staring with those penetrating, black, retracted orbs – not a shred of egg-white showing – not leaning back for idle support as would a normal man, just standing at attention as if he had at that very moment materialized into the semi-congested room. And though I do not remember much of what happened next, I do vividly recall - for the absolute uniqueness of this particular event - that he then proceeded to approach me where I sat. In the intervening years since then, I have become quite certain that he actually did sit down next to me and that we even had a lengthy conversation. My actual memories may not support this, but the certainty remains. And I am plagued by thoughts of what we might have talked about.

I woke soon thereafter to find myself upon a bus headed off to nowhere, a good simile for how I felt, knowing that the next few days would once again alter my life for the bad. There was no longer much to take away from me. I was becoming old, and my life had become quite sparse and simple. I think that the accumulation of these somewhat rare but regular occurrences, which so completely would derail and devastate any current routine ways, had acted on my subconscious to make me utterly weary and totally wary of commitments toward other people and any steady work. I preferred to be alone and uncommitted. In every sense of the word, a true loner. A part of me walked through my life as an observer only, reluctant to take on the world in any way that might provide myself with meaning. And deep inside, always that clock was ticking. Always I was waiting. Twelve years is such a long time to wait.

Especially for the worst to happen.

Which, of course, eventually it did.

This time, however, I did not at first realize what was happening.

It started with a mild sore throat and an annoying ear infection, which alone was symptomatic only of a head cold - or possibly a bit more.

It might seem anticlimactic for a loner to totally lose his voice and hearing, and in a way it was, but once the truth comes clear as to just how frequently and effectively we use these two communicating skills, the absence of them – especially both together – is experienced as a catastrophic loss, one that reverberates through your life and plagues you like an ancient boil that never heals. One is constantly reminded that he is less than able to adequately commune with others, much less able to form long-term relationships or commitments, which he previously may have thought were quite unwanted but now by comparison seemed not so bad at all. None of this would be permanently debilitating for most normal people – they would simply teach themselves somehow to adapt – but by this time I had pretty much given up on trying to improve my life. The universe seemed to want me absent from the picture, and I was beginning to agree, knowing that any improvement I could make upon my life would just be something more to take away the next time that the watching man appeared.

The final joke appeared right on schedule at seventy-two years of age.

I wanted to execute my final plans; had decided how to do so, but I did not count on being superseded by an otherworldly omniscience that could not only perceive those plans ahead of time, but also had my very worst interests closest to its heart. The trauma this time was not incidental or progressive – the stroke left me both distraught and paralyzed, and worse, completely unable to enact the misery-ending plan that I had formed. I was left instead to vegetate my remaining years, watched and cared for perfunctorily by others, as useless to the world as I was unto myself. I could think, and I could remember, and it was during this useless, listless, vegetative time that I perfected my recollections of such a strange and cursed life.

And I knew my life was cursed. The watching man made sure of that. Who else would have left the copy of the Bible by my bed, bookmarked to a passage guaranteed to send the message that my fate had once been sealed by such proscriptions. The nurse who attended to my meager wants had idly opened up the book and read – mostly to herself – the damning words from the Judas Psalm 109: *Let there be none to extend mercy unto him: neither let there be any to favour his fatherless children. Let his posterity be cut off; and in the generation following let their name be blotted out.*

After that, I simply waited for the worst to happen. After all, what could be worse than what I had wanted and waited for ever since the last time?

*****

Confined to bed, I wait. And watch.

Yesterday, I think, I turned the mighty eighty-four. At least, they brought a birthday cake into my room, ablaze with candles, along with two old nurses, and they sang my happy birthday song, after which they loaded my mouth with cake and waited for me to chew.

No way that I will be seeing ninety-six, and so I kind of sigh and watch the doorway for the watching man to enter.

Do your worst, I think.

He is standing by my bedside, studying me with those eyes of coal, and there is nothing I can read inside – neither blatant hostility, cold indifference, and most certainly not compassion. The nature of his blank-eyed stare seems to suggest a deep-held interest, but an academic one at best. And though I hope that perhaps he will renew our previous conversation, and that I might stay alert enough to finally have my ultimate questions answered; he does not, I do not, and everything just quietly comes to an end.

*****

Until I reawaken, with something like a startled click.

My mind is more alert than I have ever known. My memories, in fact, are eidetic in their clarity and super-real in the severity of their presence. I find that I can pick and choose, and in the picking and the choosing I can enter the selected memory as if it were expanded and full-blown, as if I am living out that lucid moment in my past rather than just recollecting it from the dustbin of my personal, unsatisfactory history.

And in the trance-like amazement of a sudden realization, I look down upon myself.

What I see is damning.

My arm is shiny – an oily, metallic black - and my eyes, I know, must be as flat and unexpressive as two small chunks of coal.

THE END

THAT THING UPSTAIRS

*I*t moved again.
She heard it scratching.
Not aggressively.
More like it was exploring the confines of its room – a perfect 12 x 12 – like a prisoner might explore his cell from boredom and the simple need to move his limbs. His many limbs. She tried to sense the nature of its creatured personality. As yet, she had not acquired the nerve to look upon it directly for herself, not in its finished state, although she had glimpsed the general intent behind its ill-formation - one time when bringing Uncle Frank his evening tea – and at that time she did not intuit either high aggression or any anxiety born of inordinate suppression, which might make of it something to be feared and perhaps avoided, but she somehow sensed a strange naïveté within its lonesome meanderings, its walk-about scratchings and tappings, that spoke of some awareness ignorant of any world beyond its own confining room. Which only made sense, considering it had never left the upstairs loft. But then, Uncle Frank also had not left, nor had he answered her many knockings at his door - not for two days now. And though she knew that eventually she would be obligated, she had not yet been able mentally or emotionally to crack the closed door open – not until she might somehow know better the nature of this creature that Uncle Frank had made.

Sandra knew her favorite uncle to be mad, but in a well-worn, scientifically eccentric kind of madness, the form that turns an introverted, mild-mannered professor-type into an obsessed but harmless – hopefully – wide-eyed, electrified-hair kind of scientist possessed by over-compulsive, frenzied behaviors, much like Dr. Frankenstein was personified and demonized in those really old-time movies. She had even watched as it was happening to him, tickled at first by his slow transformation into this frozen caricature of a man, then later startled by the ever-increasing luminescence glowing from his darkly haunted eyes, and then – to be quite honest about it – becoming ever more chary of his very presence in her home, even while allowing him more and more private time to indulge his scientific curiosities and evolving eccentricities.

All by himself.

Alone.

Inside that attic room upstairs.

And though the creature was now stirring about several times each day, routinely scratching its way methodically around its upstairs cage, Uncle Frank himself had gone quite silent. Sandra could sense no good in that. She fretted. And she fussed. And she began to worry, until she had no choice but to pursue an investigation, and up the stairs she climbed, albeit as slowly as her worrisome thoughts could possibly allow.

Her little knock upon the old wood door was as tentative as an over-cautious mouse peeking from its convent-shaped, baseboard hole, but the utter silence that prevailed on the other side could easily be deemed as predatory as that of the infamously-patient, masterfully-disciplined, ravenous cat.

"Uncle Frank, are you in there?" she squeaked.

The unresponsive silence felt as anticipatory and unwanted as any uninvited stare.

"Are you hungry?" she whispered, upset by that particular choice of words.

She tried to turn the door handle, and to her dismay it turned. The little jiggling sound it made was echoed by a barely discernible scuttling sound on the other side, as if something shy and wary had inadvertently stepped back one or two small paces. The timidity of the sound emboldened her a little more. She pushed the door ajar, if only just beyond a meager crack, and peered inside, just in time to see something quite mechanical scurry behind the open bathroom door. Something much too big, however, to have made such a timid tapping noise.

But her eyes were also taken by the mess inside.

Yes, this small room was an addendum to the loft – an attic, really – with the basin washroom and this tiny office separated from all the rest by just an old and battered, tattered, gray cloth curtain, and – as everyone knows - attics are notorious for their junkiness. Still, Uncle Frank with all his scattered mental nature was ironically rather meticulous about his work and extremely conscientious about the fastidiousness of his surroundings. A place for everything, and everything in its place. The best of mottos. Especially in this place - what he liked to call his workroom. The rest of the attic might be a junk-filled, messy storeroom, and might be allowed always to remain so, but now it had certainly over-spilled its boundaries. The more conditioned part of Sandra was immediately inclined to begin cleaning up the mess – the shredded bits of heavily-inked-upon notebook paper, the oily newspaper left squarely open as if to housebreak a newly learning pet, the stray metallic nuts and bolts strewn about like chicken seed, not to mention the rather unusual rusty stains now decorating the faux-wood floor as if Pollack had made a visitation – but Uncle Frank was not a vital member of this mess, and she dearly hoped he was perhaps sleeping deeply in the farther room upon his favorite and familiar lumpy couch.

Tis a consummation devoutly to be wished.

Another unfortunate choice of words to bedevil her now anxious and addlepated mind.

Sandra did not call out her Uncle's name. She did not wish to bestir whatever creature lurked behind the bathroom door, not necessarily because she felt wary – which she did – but more because the creature displayed such a wariness of its own in response to her immediate and impending presence. Instead, she made her way across the cluttered floor, around the soiled newsprint - being hyper-careful not to step upon the stray nuts and bolts; even more careful to avoid the rusty stains – and then, pulling back the too-still curtain hanging somnolently like a shroud, she peered into the darkness that lay impenetrably just beyond.

"Uncle Frank?" she whispered.

At this, there came a tiny sound, but not from the dark in front of her.

From behind her.

She flinched a little and pulled the curtain entirely open, letting in only a modicum of light, which did almost nothing to lighten up the lengthy loft itself, nor her own profound sense of burdensome foreboding. Uncle Frank was certainly not a sleeping burden occupying the ancient couch, though that is where she promptly plopped herself for the foreseeable next few moments, disinclined to venture farther into the shadows - even though she was fairly certain that was where she would find a recently expired Frank, perhaps the victim of a stroke or a sudden and massive heart attack. And no, she did not consider for a second that she might revive him back to life; the room was much too still for that.

Oddly, she began tentatively planning her own near-future.

The equally tentative and hesitantly approaching taps beyond the curtain did not immediately intrude, so she was rather startled to suddenly see a face poised expectantly at the now open entry to the loft. Two faces, actually. Little girls. Baby girls, really, but poised up high as if on older bodies. Absently, she noted that their eyes were closed - more like doll faces when their plastic heads are lowered gently into pretend sleep by a young pretend-mother's pretend-lullaby. And though their pale plastic skin and purplish bruise-infused lips made them look as dead as dead could be – or just not very real (as dolls typically are not supposed to be) – something in the manner of their attention told Sandra that this was not quite completely true.

And then, regrettably, her brain put it all together.

She gave a little gasp.

She had already pushed herself upright against the couch, packing all the lumps, but still she pushed back some more.

For, this was the creature Uncle Frank had made.

She already knew that perfectly well, of course. What else could it be? Certainly not two girls, or even dolls. But all that she had seen when peering in that one time before were those tippy-tappy, multi-segmented, insectoid metallic legs machining themselves around the room in an absurdly awkward, tentative, naïve manner - as she recalled – and there had been only four connected at the time. Now there were six; not quite a spider; another thought she immediately regretted.

"Oh, Uncle Frank," she murmured. "You've been a busy boy."

Even as she was blindly studied by those two blank and closed-eyed girlish faces, Sandra studied them in return with the kind of indiscreet stare a man saves only for a woman. And she was taken by three immediate observations, though she could not declare which of them disturbed her the most: the robotic, carapace-looking, cone-shaped helmet somehow glued atop both heads at once, with some very peculiar small-pipe extension perched like a scorpion tail above their brows, as if it were perhaps a small microphone they might speak into should their mouths be forced to open; the distended abdomen – exactly like the aforementioned spider's – ballooning like a pregnant ulcer, weirdly, but also rather appropriately to the rear, as if it were some kind of over-exposed added bustle; or that anachronistic warrior skirt – reminiscent of a Roman's kilt – placed suggestively, if not quite modestly, where any private parts might lie.

Other than that, as the staring man might say, she was all legs.

When Sandra noticed that the bloated abdomen - unlike the other attributes – was biological in nature, even to the point of sporting a rash of tiny, bristly hairs, she made her final choice regarding what most disturbed her about Uncle Frank's creation. But when she saw that bulbous appendage begin pulsing in a fit of organic rhythmic ripples, she gagged and had to bring her hand up to her mouth. Sandra, quite suddenly, did not feel well at all.

An errant thought intruded to keep her from disgorging a tiny bit of bile: the widely-pleated skirt was colored dirty rose and might have been her mother's, stored and inappropriately retrieved from some old attic trunk.

"Oh really, Uncle Frank. How could you?" she asked, rhetorically.

Maybe it was that internal maternal mental reference, however, that made her hunker down into herself, into that familiar female place where everything turns simply practical, and address herself to the obvious if imponderable distress of what stood expectantly before her, knowing that once again her choice of words had betrayed her current greatest fear.

"Oh, my dear," she whispered. "You simply cannot be."

But whether Sandra was speaking categorically or existentially, she herself could not be truly sure.

That is when the dolls' eyes opened.

This time, 'Oh!' was all that she could manage before Sandra was forced to swallow something bitter.

She had not honestly considered the thing to be alive. Certainly not in any pulsing, organic way. And most assuredly not with any volition to open up its presumably non-organic eyes. Forcing herself to peer into them more closely, Sandra did satisfy her increasing though morbidly stressed curiosity enough to know that those two pairs of eyes were still dead, or more accurately – not alive. Then again, something proximate behind them did seem to be aware. Something in the posture of the heads – a kind of alert stillness – gave the appearance of someone – something – listening. And maybe that is why Sandra began talking directly to the creature with a tone that sounded – even to her understanding nature – condescending, if not quite patronizing.

"So, little one. Err ... ones," she corrected, twitching her own eyes between the two, wondering if one body with two heads should be considered one or two, even in her confusion imagining two brains inside the heads – one for each, of course – but her thoughts were not that precise.

"Where is Uncle Frank?" she asked, as if she might expect from them a spoken answer.

And though the dreadful scratching in return might have been some errant hexagonal nut loosening or tightening upon a rusty bolt, she really felt the thing was attempting thereby to talk, and she knew that she possessed many tiny hairs upon the nape of her own neck, because they were all abruptly standing up.

"What are you?" she whispered, so softly she kind of scared herself.

At this, the creature approached more closely, if only two or three more steps, depending on the number of spear-tipped legs that had actually engineered the move – spiderlike and mechanical – in her direction. When those dead-doll eyes blinked, Sandra knew that somehow she was understood, and that did not sit particularly well with her. But when that protruding coupler pipe extension hovering above the helmet began to emit a bit of static from its acorn-shaped, fine-meshed tip, Sandra gave up all pretense for any understanding of her own. Finally, well knowing that she had put this off for way too long, Sandra craned her neck to look around behind her, far back into the loft, and stood up from the couch, prepared to discover for herself just where Uncle Frank had gone. The creature seemed to sense this, and with a gesture so intimately private as to register as surreal, she tapped Sandra with a foot – or hand – and pointed into the darkness.

Sandra sort of shuffled through the cluttered loft, reluctant to find the body she knew must still be there … somewhere. The chilliness in the attic must have prevented the smell of death from emanating everywhere, but fortunately for her, she did not entertain that particularly dreadful thought. She was thinking more about the strangeness of what tapped along beside her, and she was trying oh so hard to be so very quiet about her thinking, because she was wondering how exactly she was going to dismantle and destroy Uncle Frank's bizarre creation. Just behind that thought was another one that she could not yet approach: *Would it even let her?*

When she felt the creature pause, she stopped. It was looking at something on the floor – or that is where the heads were bent – but she could not ascertain the outline of a body, or the bulk necessary to define one. And yet, the strange sadness suggested by the creature's sullen pose made her look more closely, made her kneel down and make a desultory and half-hearted sweeping search with one outstretched arm and a slightly flailing hand. What she found was hard, and several, and caused her brow to furrow.

"That is me," the creature croaked, metallically and rustically.

"Huh," Sandra muttered, preoccupied at the moment with preventing any further thoughts from entering a similar attic in her brain.

"What's left," the creature added, with a bit less rust this time.

When the curtain in Sandra's brain drifted partially aside – perhaps due to that small breath caused from something talking – her eyes clicked over to the side like dolls' eyes planted sideways and thus became misaligned. Her mouth, too, dropped a little open.

"Frank?" she croaked, sounding also like rusty metal, but now omitting the honorific title of relationship.

"Sorry, my dear."

At last, Sandra succumbed to her over-stimulated senses and passed out on the floor.

*****

Of course, she awakened on the couch.

With the creature looking down on her. Solicitously? She could not tell.

Sandra slowly and ponderously pulled herself up to sitting, but she could not bring herself to raise her head.

"Uncle Frank," she moaned into her hands. "Whatever did you do?"

Silence.

"Are you really in there?" she asked, cringing even as she said the words.

Silence.

"How?" she asked.

This time there followed a lengthy pause, and then the wretched sound of rust.

"I don't know."

Sandra blinked her ragged gaze up into the two dead faces. And though she would not have believed that she held the capacity to ask, she did.

"What about those bones?"

"Those are mine."

"Yes," she said. "But why?"

The creature shifted on its robotic legs, as if trying to find a more comfortable stance in which to settle, but not quite succeeding.

"When I awoke," the rusty voice said from the tiny little speaker, "I was very, very hungry."

"Hungry? How could such a thing ... how could you be hungry?"

"I just was."

"But how could you even eat?"

The creature – or more properly understood, Uncle Frank – lifted up a leg and said, "Through the feet. I can eat things ... or absorb them ... through my feet.

"Oh god," Sandra moaned, and then just went silent.

"The food goes to my stomach."

"Shut up, Frank."

"And out the rear," he added.

"Shut ... the ... holy ... fuck ... up."

"It's only liquid," he said.

74

"Frank!"

"My dear, I am so sorry."

"I need to clean," she said, apropos of nothing, and certainly not making any move to suggest that she would actually follow through.

And then they just continued sitting there in utter silence for a most considerable length of time, each presumably lost in his or her own thoughts. Sandra found it nigh impossible to connect hers into any kind of neural train that might lead her on a rail out of this desecrated station, and who could say what kind of thoughts might wander through the heads of two dead dolls, redundant as that might sound. Neither made a sound; neither spoke a word; neither seemed to exist beyond the ever-eternal moment. As evening fell outside, matching the constant dimness of the attic, one could easily wonder what might befall these wretched two now commiserating without speaking, and thinking without thought.

The only sound to break the silence was a rusty nut unbolting.

"Sandy?"

"Yes, Uncle Frank."

"I'm hungry."

"What?"

"I am so very, very hungry.

THE END

THE WOODS GIRL

I don't know why she treated me differently from the rest. Perhaps we all just need one untouchable friend in this abundantly lonely world. I have thought about her often across the many years that now comprise the memories of my life, and when I do, my thoughts about the woods girl are as clear to me as the mountain air on a crispy sunny day, and my recall is sharper than with any other recollection I may choose to bring into my mind. And every time I do think about her, I am inclined to wonder: *Is she still there?* And always the answer I must compulsively assume is right remains the same: *Of course she is.* But then, as a most natural extrapolation from such a supernatural consideration, I ask myself: *Should I go back?* And of course I always answer: *No, I must not.* She gave me her fairest warning and, seriously, I listened. But now, now I am reconsidering, and that surprises me. Maybe I am rethinking such a fatal visit in these my later years because … well, now I have nothing left to lose except my heart. And maybe because I am quite convinced that she is calling me to return.

Many years ago, so much closer to the beginning of my life than now, at an age just before I reached young manhood, one uneventful day I found myself walking in the woods, alone. A young fellow such as myself, of a more cerebral and moody temperament than most his peers, finds a certain productive pleasure in simply meandering along a highly shadowed road, leading through a forest of quietly observant trees, beneath their benedictive branches with their susurrantly whispering leaves. Thus, as I proceeded on my aimless, road-determined walk, my thoughts were mostly idle and likely preoccupied with trying to define the nature of such a marvelous ambivalence towards any particular destination, whether in my life itself or specifically within those woods, neither of which could claim for me a passion I had yet to find. Because I was indifferent and unprepared, the woods girl appeared to me at first to be a kind of vision projected by my subtly yearning thoughts, for her presence in those woods – sitting there beside the road on what appeared to be her luggage - although not particularly unusual in itself, was made more so by her oddly statue-like, still-life posture, poised and deeply meditative, as if she were supremely meant to be waiting there - just like that - forever.

A slender shaft of sunlight shone down upon her pale, delicate hand resting calmly on an aproned knee, the apron an adornment to the overly modest, old-fashioned dress she wore. I could not see her face for the long and straight brown hair concealing her obviously youthful profile, but something in her pose convinced me she was pretty. And, somewhat delighted at my presumed, unexpected good fortune, I approached her with the utmost intention to be charming.

Eventually, I came to stand before her. She did not at first look up, nor move her hand, nor with any physical indication or change in posture acknowledge that I had indeed intruded, for my charming inclination was to stand inordinately close, so that for the moment I was simply looking down upon her slightly lowered head. By my proximity and my silence, I hoped to make her initiate a conversation – or at least a greeting – if only by the intimidation my standing there imposed, implying a certain subjection on her part and a certain mastery on mine. I was young. But, with a softness and a sadness that pierced my then uncrenellated heart, she spoke first.

"So, you've come."

Enigmatic and elliptic words at best, but ones that sent a distinctly pleasant shiver down my spine and made my undefended heart quiver at the smallest sound of expectancy contained therein, with - might one hope? – an intended if yet unspoken welcome.

"Yes," I said, not nearly meeting the requirements of charm to which I had aspired. But she responded warmly to my voice, and as she raised her face to mine, she smiled, although with a closed-lips smile that only served to enhance the incredible beauty and sadness showing in her very pretty and delicately pale face.

"The one I must not touch," she whispered, which admittedly set me back a pace, if only in my head. And I did what most of us charming guys end up doing: I stood there quietly, looking stupid.

"Why don't you sit?" she offered, patting the unnervingly small open space beside her.

"Isn't that your luggage?"

"Not quite," she said. "Don't worry. It should hold you, too."

As I settled myself down next to her - awkwardly as it turned out, my knees projecting too high upwards toward my face, for I am rather tall and lanky, and forcing me to wrap my arms around them as if hugging myself for warmth, in turn causing me to hunch forward slightly in a most non-flattering counterpoint to her perfect posture - I asked the girl her name.

"Caroline," she responded. "With a long I," she said, then added, "As in pine."

"I know what a long I is," I said.

"Oh, you have absolutely no idea," she murmured, in her enigmatic way.

"Mine is John," I responded. "As in yawn," I added, meaning to be funny in a charming, self-deprecating way.

"No doubt," she said, refusing the giggle for which I had been fishing.

We sat there for many minutes – it seemed – in awkward silence; I more uncomfortable than she, but something for which I was rather well prepared by a lifetime maybe brief to most but long to me of just such uncomfortable silences with almost all my peers and definitely all of my more casual-type acquaintances. I was not big on chit-chat, nor did I have any adequate context by which I might make an entrée into even idle conversation with such a girl, except of course for the glaringly obvious one declaring itself so loudly by our continued silence and oddly juxtaposed sitting postures.

"Caroline, can I ask you something?" I asked.

That elusive giggle almost happened then, but did not quite make a full appearance, instead manifesting itself as a kind of gentle smirk to stretch her still closed lips sideways, and also as a gentle glint from her surreptitious, sideways-glancing eyes.

"Gee, Yawn, let me guess. You're wondering what a young girl like me, dressed like some smarmy acolyte or school marm, is doing out here in these woods alone, sitting on her luggage, her only piece of luggage, also dated from somewhere way too distant in the past, waiting for, what?, some miraculously appearing bus to take me on?" And though her words fairly reeked of sardonic sarcasm, her tone somehow did not. She actually made it sound like a fair and viable question. Still, I did not know how I might respond.

"Time to tell my story," she said, reading my indecision as if she had done this a time or two before. "John, do you believe in curses?"

"Curses?" I repeated, thinking I sounded like a dimwit.

"Well, apparently the day that I was born my bruja of a grandmother, upon observing me all wrapped up into a tight and pretty packaged little bundle, declared: *That girl is going to steal all the young men's hearts,* and then crossed herself as mightily as any peasant woman would if suddenly bedeviled by the unwavering gaze directed at her from some old crone's maleficent evil eye. She claimed several times as I was growing up that those poor young men were waiting out there in droves just to be victimized by me. My mother would chuckle at her ravings, pleased that I was indeed growing up to be such a pretty little thing, but letting her own mother's repeated crossings act as adequate protection against any inherent curse automatically inflicted upon such impeccable beauty."

This girl, with her immodest if impressively accurate powers of self-assessment, seemed to be testing me for a wickedly tender gullible streak, or at least a minor weakness for the more teasing gender.

"You are a pretty girl," I said, managing a little bit of charm at last.

"I am not," she stated flatly, "a girl anymore."

"And that is what I'm trying to tell you," she added.

"Go on," I said, gesturing with my hand.

"When I reached young womanhood," she continued, "looking precisely as you see me now, I did steal a young man's heart. To my knowledge at the time, he was my first, though I suspect in truth that he was not; that I had indeed made unwilling suitors of many men, of many ages, some of whom should have been thoroughly disgusted with themselves. It was not a difficult thing to do. It came to me quite naturally. In fact, I merely smiled at them. But this boy whose heart I thought to steal first began the fulfillment of my previously only imaginary curse."

Although I was disturbed by the implications in her words, initially I sort of mentally wrote them off to exaggeration, or at least a more imaginative way of telling what was in truth a typical and therefore a necessarily mundane story of youth eventually coming into age. Like me, I guess. If so, however, I found that I could not predict the final destination of her story, nor could I ascertain even with my more cerebral bent the connection of my sitting there with her to the words she had spoken first upon our meeting: *So, you've come.* Already it seemed I wanted to be someone special to her, perhaps even her own Prince Charming. At that young age I suppose I still had some imaginative exaggeration issues of my own with which to cope.

"When I had finished with the boy," she spoke on, "my bruja grandma made to me a gift of the antiquated luggage you feel beneath your butt. 'You will need this for your collection,' she said. I asked her if I was going somewhere – perhaps I was meant to travel, you see – but she only responded that I must now proceed into the woods to fulfill the destiny of my fate. Some such inflated nonsense, anyway. And of course I thought that she was kidding; sending such a beauty into the forest. It fairly reeked of classic fairy tales. I was waiting for her admonishment about accepting gifts and such from strangers, but she only gave me one: 'There will come wandering along, once in every now and then,' and she actually spoke like that, 'a boy whom you must not touch; whose heart you must not steal. To him, you must simply tell your story as you know it to be true.'"

At this point, I realized just how gullible I had become while listening to this girl telling me in her own words: *I could easily seduce you, but I shall not.* She must have sensed my immediate attraction to her youthfully feminine attributes and come up with this fanciful tale to soften my ultimate and guaranteed rejection. I could have been resentful, I guess, but I actually felt more amused, and maybe just a bit relieved. I mean, such a strange girl sitting all by herself on a suitcase in the woods? This was really just a bit too much, after all. Perhaps she often played this game for some peculiar amusement of her own. In any case, I smiled, acquiescent and willing to have been the easily targeted mark in her little game of con the boy. She must have sensed my own amusement then, for she suddenly broke into sarcastic laughter of her own, still not smiling, but certainly taking some sweet merriment at my expense. And yet, I had misinterpreted her gay response.

"You do not believe me, of course," she laughed. "It is indeed not a story meant either for quick acceptance or belief."

Something in her burst of laughter alerted me at last – producing the same sudden, brilliant clarity one might experience from a splash of ice cold water - to a precarious present danger resulting from my previous submissive if slightly awkward equanimity; my bland acceptance; nay, my predictable masculine eagerness to aid a pretty girl in distress. For in her laughter I heard not the softly ringing bells of youthful romance but the crackling, exploding snaps of a bitter-dry woods engulfed by raging, angry flames. Those flames were mirrored twins dancing in her eyes; staring, glaring, at me now. As I rose from where I had been crouching beside her on the suitcase, her head and gaze followed my lengthy unfolding upward. Still, she did not smile, not even with the grimace I suspected might lay there in patience waiting for me, a smile you could almost see lurking just behind her lips.

"Don't you want to see my collection, sir?" she asked me, coyly.

"Okay," I said, and I am not even a little bit sure why, because I most certainly did not.

She stood up then and stepped back one short pace from her luggage before bending down to unlock the snaps, affording me an automatic if surreptitious and appreciative view of her behind, while the old fashioned dress flowed lovely down her curves.

"Naughty boys," she murmured, as if in judgement of us all.

"Here they are," she said, and stood aside.

I shall just admit it now. I gasped. And not at all in any good way. Although what I was seeing then failed to register completely upon my comprehension, the literal nature of her story somehow had fertilized my brain toward instant recognition of the objects now within my vision. At first I thought they might be plums, ripe and purple and tantalizing in their fullness, but really I knew better. Right from the start, I must have known better. And even if I had somehow managed to deceive myself right then and there, the deception would have ended when I saw that they were sickly pulsing, looking suspiciously like eggs about to hatch, the small inhabitants pecking at their mucous shells in rhythmical, repetitious, pulsating pokes, as if by such measured metronomics alone they might escape the sticky bonds of their entrapment.

The plums lived.

My hand rose up to my mouth, bile rose up into my throat, and my feet shuffled backwards independent of my or their volition. Caroline shook her head at my regretful but fully predictable reaction, and simply said, "You should go." When I hesitated just a bit, she rephrased her words, "You must go. You must not come back. Not ever."

And I believed her.

I probably grunted some inarticulate, mutilated form of fond farewell, then I turned around too slowly, entered into some brand new kind of mental haze, and began to trudge my way reluctantly – if only in appearance - down that singularly directed road. I should have continued on, never looking back, but when in all your years have you ever seen someone capable of doing that? Not me, that's for sure. Not then.

Not far enough down the road, I stopped and turned around. I looked back. The vision was the same as when I had first arrived, maybe several lifetimes of mine ago. The young girl sat still upon her luggage, her posture perfect but also radiant with a lingering, eternal sense of sadness. My Caroline. Except, her pale hand no longer rested upon her aproned knee. No shaft of sunlight filtered down. Instead, in the shadow of her open palm sat a most perfect plum, or perhaps an apple.

"Oh dear god," I prayed. "Please let it be."

And then she raised the apple to her mouth and took one long and savoring bite, then raised her eyes to lock on mine.

And then, after all our time together, finally she smiled.

****

Had I not turned around, had I not felt the desperation of her smile upon myself as a deeply embedded physical and emotional compulsion, the remainder of my life would surely have been much different. I never married. I never encountered a girl like Caroline again, she who left her personal mark of ownership upon me as surely as her own grandmother had eternally scarred her with that ill-considered curse. A curse designed for beauty. A curse meant for the hearts of men. A curse destined, perversely, just for me.

There is something that women do not, perhaps cannot, understand. The most ravishing smile in the world is not one made from irresistible beauty or stratagems of seduction. These have their marked effect upon men, certainly they do, but they do not possess their souls. They do not steal their hearts. They do not compel them into forsaking an entire life. No, the only smile that can accomplish that is one of sadness brought about by a void of emptiness so deep that one cannot perceive an ending; cannot see to the bottom of the depths of genuine loneliness and despair.

Caroline was genuinely alone.

The sadness of her smile was therefore desperately alluring.

I came so close to returning to her that very day. And maybe that is what she truly wanted and intended for me ... for us. How can I know? The yearning in her eyes seemed fully comparable to mine, despite the sound of angry reality hidden in her voice. I know she was not the young maiden she feigned herself to be. And yet, the maiden was in there too. I shake my head at these memories now, as clear to me today as when they happened to me then, and I just sit here staring out the window into the woods, thinking I can hear her calling, can see her waiting, can see her smiling.

Ready to steal my heart.

And all I want, have wanted my entire life, is to hear her murmur one more time:

So, you've come.

And for me to answer:

Yes.

THE END

GREAT UNCLE JACK

*U*ncle Jack was great. He would make us laugh by telling Sis and me that he was a prisoner in the war and that they tried to make him talk by stretching him on *The Rack*. When they threw acid in his face to shut him up, he always declared that he yelled back, "You can't have it both ways, guys!" When we were smaller – and we always were – he would settle us somewhere on his massive lap in order to tell us these really funny stories. One time he told me that he had been raised up by redwood trees, and later when he took me to see his "birthplace" he made me say "hi" to his Mum and Dad. We even took a photo. He asked me if I saw the obvious resemblance, saying that he took mostly after Mum.

I never knew when he was being serious.

His face was kind of smeared, like it had melted, so it wasn't like you could look him in the eyes; you know, to see if he was kidding. His mouth was melted too, and so he mostly mumbled when he talked, which made us guess at what he said. His head hung low and crooked, but we couldn't tell if he was always kind of sad, or naturally humble, or if his neck was just permanently broken. His arms were as long as I was tall, but they still didn't reach down to his knees, so that rack thing probably did end up stretching him out a bit. One leg was twisted all the way around, with an elephant foot like a stump, and he always wore a suit of black.

Our Uncle Jack was great.

Jack came to us by way of Mum and Dad one year before that tree thing, when Sis and I were exactly that much younger. It seems ironic to me now, or maybe just highly coincidental, that our parents passed on soon after Jack's arrival, and thus it was we found ourselves taken under his protective care. We did not tell anyone about the death of Mum and Dad; Jack did not think that would be a good idea, which, now that I think about it, does seem perhaps a wee bit odd. Instead, we buried them out in the woods beneath a tree on which we placed two small wooden crosses and listened to Jack mumble on a bit about the abundance of their "plenitudinous" good graces. As I recall, a tear may have rolled its lugubrious way down his melted face, but of that I cannot be sure. In any case, we were not all that sad, my Sis and I, because Uncle Jack told really good and funny stories.

I think I mentioned that.

The year following my parents' death was mostly good. I took on the chores of Mum – cooking, cleaning, tending to the fractious hens – while Jack took on the responsibilities of Dad – hunting game for meat, fixing up the homestead, and axing wood to burn. Sis could be a nuisance, calling me out to play when there was still so much serious work left to be attended, but eventually she learned to occupy herself by disappearing for long stretches at a time into the woods to play. And of course there were all those fabulous stories told to us while sitting perched so perilously high up on Uncle Jack's bony knees. Sometimes Sis might grimace to herself, but I was thoroughly delighted by the gruesome pictures Jack would paint, for he seemed to come from a world that was dangerous and mean, and the sardonic way he had of telling us about his chronic misfortunes always made me laugh.

Once he told us about this traveling circus show with a vicious bunch of tiny men who tried to break his "stilts." When they brought him to his knees and he was forced to waddle like a duck, they climbed aboard his back looking to take a jaunty ride. Then they whipped him to go faster, and he yelled, "You can't have it both ways, guys!" Which seemed to be his answer for almost everything, I guess. But most of all, I liked to listen to his dreadful war stories, especially when the war was done and he was left to wander all alone across a deliciously desolated landscape looking for food because he was literally starving. He told us that his body had forgotten how to hold onto the little food he ate, and that was why he remained so thin today; or, as he called it: *lanky*. And once, when he was feeling quite confessional, he admitted that maybe he had even consumed one or two recently deceased bodies ... or maybe even three.

That story made me laugh for days.

Perhaps because of his dreadfully morbid past, Uncle Jack never seemed to be too surprised at anything unusual that happened to him in the here and now. Not that a whole lot of unusual things happened out here in our particular neck of the woods, but we had our moments. Often, I would see Jack grab his ax and wander into those same woods in search of game. Mostly rabbits, but sometimes something bigger, like a fox or a reckless little pig left running wild – meat for our table, anyway. So as not to use up all our chickens, especially the ones good for laying eggs. I was quite used to seeing Jack return with new blood dripping from his ax blade and something furry dangling from his hand, and boy would my mouth begin to water. Sometimes, when Sis would start to wander off towards the woods to play, Uncle Jack would admonish her by saying, "Watch out for those damn bears." Which made me wonder why we never had any bear meat set out on the table for our supper, but then I just always assumed that there might finally come a day.

Although I tried, I could not lift Jack's heavy ax, so it remained always in the corner by the shed. But I could lift the hatchet, the one used for cutting the heads off of our chickens, the ones meant for dinner, and I used to pretend a lot that I was fighting those bears hiding in the woods. One day, I came walking back from the woods holding the bear-killing hatchet by my side, only to see Uncle Jack walking towards me with his game-killing ax by his side, and we both just stopped to stare at one another until I smiled. He kind of shook his head a little and said, "We need to talk." I said okay and set my hatchet down and together we walked into the house, where I climbed up onto his lap and he began to tell me a different story.

"Your sister has gone missing," he said, by way of introduction.

"Again?" I asked.

"Not like that," he said. "I mean she went off to play and has not come home again."

"She always does that," I said. "How long has she been gone this time?"

"Two days," he said.

I had to laugh at that. I couldn't help myself.

"Mebbe a bear ett her up," I said, faking a backwoods drawl.

"Maybe," he said, "but we need to go out and look for her."

"Okay," I said brightly as I climbed down from his knee.

The day outside was amazingly bright, like one of those first shining days of spring that you read about in books. Even in the woods, the brilliant sunshine came pouring down through the tree breaks as if it were raining golden goodness on our heads, or some such foolish stuff. The remaining morning dewdrops on the leaves sparkled with reflected sunlight, and I suppose that the birds were probably singing. I was reminded of an old Easter morning when we used to search for stuff buried in the ground. Despite all this, I remained my cheery self as we sauntered into the woods to look for missing Sis - Uncle Jack and I.

And I suppose it was the brightness of the day that made it so easy to see her blood when we eventually came upon it, a rather large pool of congealing liquid settled – rather ironically, I must say – beneath the very tree where Mum and Dad were buried. Uncle Jack and I stood staring at the dark plum pool as if it might begin to talk, Jack with his furrowed brow and I humming a little nursery rhyme to myself. To liven up the mood a little more, I offered an obvious observation.

"I guess that old bear left nothing of her behind," I said.

Uncle Jack gave me the strangest look.

"Not even one teeny weeny bone," I added.

Jack grabbed my hand and together we headed on back home, me feeling like I was being herded reluctantly along like some recalcitrant little puppy, but I felt happy nonetheless. I was hoping to get some cold milk and listen to more stories from Uncle Jack. But when we got home, Jack was acting strange. He was not in any mood to tell me stories, so I went outside to play with my crazy clutch of chickens. I gathered them all around, told them to quiet their insidious clucking, and I began to tell them the story about Sis and Uncle Jack. And, I must admit, I must have told it rather well, because the chickens all began to chuckle.

The days passed normally after that. Jack and I returned to our regular routine, but because Sis no longer participated in our after-dinner storytelling, I would switch back and forth up there on Uncle Jack's bony knees in order not to overburden him. I think he appreciated that consideration. The funniest story that he ever told me was about the time he spent working at this orphanage where a whole bunch of kids suddenly went missing. After the circus, he said he found it very hard to get a job, but there was this old time penitentiary-looking building where the town locked up its abandoned kids, mostly boys, and since the lads were so unruly and caused so much trouble when left unmanaged, the townspeople found it incumbent - if notoriously difficult - to retain some extra help.

They were glad to get Jack.

He told me that the conditions in the orphanage were just terrible. He said the beds were made of broken wood and rusty springs and covered mildewed straw, full of bugs and mice and stuff, and that several kids had to sleep in a single bed together. The whole place was dark and dirty; the food was rank and rotten; and the children were only let out to play but once a week, out in a yard where they had buried horses who had grown too old for riding. I thought he might be kidding, but like I said, I could never tell when Uncle Jack was serious.

But, he said, the strangest thing of all was when most those kids went missing, when perhaps half of all who lived there just disappeared one day. This happened on the one day they had been let out in the yard to play. Jack was supposed to be watching over them, to see that they didn't get into too much trouble, and especially that they didn't start digging up those dead and rotting horses, as they were much too prone to do when unattended, but the toilets in the basement had backed themselves up and flooded the whole first floor with shit – that's what he said – and he had to clean it up. After describing that part, he had to wait for me to stop laughing before he could finish with the rest.

Anyway, when he was done with cleaning up, outside he went to herd the bunch of kids back inside, and that is when he found that most of them were gone. The kids who were still playing in the yard had no idea where the rest had gone to, or at least they were too scared to say. And while the townsfolk figured that the lost boys must have run away, none of them were ever seen again, not one, and that seemed really, really odd. Jack said he didn't stay there long after that. But that was his best story ever, and I kissed him on the cheek for telling it.

Even lying in my bed that night, while trying to go to sleep, I would start thinking about that story once again, and I couldn't help but laugh.

I really loved Uncle Jack.

That is why what happened next bothered me so much.

*****

So. There I am standing out in our cluttered backyard one afternoon. I have been playing with the chickens. They are scattered all around me. I am wearing my best dress, the one with the little bows and ribbons and the lacy little sleeves. I have my dressy shoes on, the white ones with the buckles. I have a pretty little bonnet on my head. I am holding the hatchet in my hand. When suddenly around the corner of the house comes Uncle Jack holding his ax tightly in both his hands. He is striding toward me with a guilty angry look upon his face, not a friendly look at all. He lumbers to the side a bit because of that strangely twisted leg of his, and then he stops and stomps his hard elephant foot upon the ground. His melted face begins to twitch, and the next thing I know Uncle Jack begins to yell at me. At me! And what he yells at me is not the least bit funny.

"You are a nasty little girl," he says. "A nasty, dirty little tramp."

And though I feel an inappropriate surge of pleasure, I know that he does not mean these things to be taken in a good way.

"I know you killed your Mum and Dad," he yells. "You chopped them up and tried to hide them in the woods."

Uncle Jack is almost spitting, he's so mad.

"I didn't turn you in," he says. "I thought I could protect you and make you well. Then you killed your sister."

Such horrible accusations are spilling from his mouth. I cannot believe he is saying these awful things to me. What's worse, I think he is the one who killed my Mum and Dad and chopped them up. And I only said that bit about the bear because I thought he was the one who also chopped up little Sis. He should be ashamed of himself, saying these dreadful things to me. I feel the hatchet in my hand begin to shake. But Uncle Jack is not yet done with his vicious harrangue against me.

"And now, look at what you've done," he says. "You've slaughtered all the chickens. We have nothing left to eat. Your finest dress is all splattered with blood and guts. It's totally ruined. What is wrong with you! You're just a girl, but you are nothing but a monster!"

I am so shocked, I cannot speak. Uncle Jack has never spoken to me like this before. It is awful. And I just know he killed all these chickens and left them headless here like this just to upset me more. And I am upset. I am actually crying. The tears are running down my cheeks in rivers. And I feel the hatchet in my hand begging to terminate this horrible harassment. His words are so terrible to me. I must stop them now.

And in his eyes I see the same determination. He holds his lethal, traitorous bloody ax in both his hands and he takes a step towards me. I grab my only protection in my two hands and I take a step towards him. We mean to finish this here and now.

*****

I felt so glad when we put our differences behind us.

That little episode in the yard really put me off my stride, and I was pleased to return to our more pleasurable - if decidedly more mundane - household routines. Especially I liked the moment right after dinner when I would again climb onto Uncle Jack's high lap and listen raptly to his stories. Understandably, I still had to interpret Jack's less-than-perfect diction in order to benefit from his tales, but he still entertained me by talking about those maleficent events with which the Universe had seemed overly compelled to burden him.

The only time he thought the Universe had smiled on him was when Mum and Dad offered to take him in. They knew that he would love us girls – me and Sis – and that our life for him would help to overcome the worst misfortunes of his life. He could help out with the chores, and his inclusion in our family would overcome any ill effects that such a secluded upbringing might devolve onto the children. Perhaps he could tell us stories; that he might be able to make us laugh.

And so he did.

To his credit, Jack only asked me once why I chose to leave his head upon the kitchen table, but I patiently explained that it was the only way to feed him dinner and still keep his lanky body on the chair where I could climb up to listen to his stories. I mean, I couldn't keep lugging him from place to place now, could I?

Or, like I then summarized for him, "You can't have it both ways, guy."

He laughed heartily at that.

Uncle Jack, you see, was just so very great.

THE END

OUR LITTLE TOWN

*I*n our little town, I grew up believing the devil keeps his eye on us all.

Nothing but the dead and dying live here now.

I am one of them.

Since you seem to have wandered in here on your own, perhaps I can show you around a bit, give you the lay of the land, so to speak. Your timing is impeccable. The others can't wait to get their hands on you. Ha! A little joke of mine. Never mind. Follow me. Please ignore the fly swarms. That's Billie's broken bike ditched up over there against our useless fence. Ignore the warning signs up ahead; they're old too. And most of them dark birds hoverin' over everything ... they won't bother you much; not just yet. Yeah, pretty sure. That's my house. The roof's a mess, ain't it! Come inside, though. We can check out them windmills later on, maybe take a ride on some torn sails. And we still gotta explore our little graveyard. Ha! Sorry. 'Nother joke. The crosses are everywhere, don't you see?

C'mon, I'll race ya up to the back door.

Watch your step there, old girl. I'm Chuck, by the way. Yeah, I know ... Becky. Love the pearls. Let's head upstairs. You can see our entire town from up there. Don't worry. The steps should hold you fine. Just watch that big ol' hole on your way up.

In here, Becks. This is my room. Come on over to the window. Oops ... yeah ... go on, kick that busted head outta your way ... mind the dust ... come here, you can see out this shattered pane ... lookit all them rows and rows and rows of corn. Well, it was corn once upon a time, I guess. Still kinda pretty, though. All them droopy, weedy brown stalks just standing out there like dead soldiers too tired to march. I love watching them. Can do it for hours. That there is Miles' place. And off to the side ... can't quite see it ... that's where Schuster hangs out ... we'll catch up to him later. Sorry, Becky, we don't get too many of the female persuasion hereabouts. But lookit it this way: you're gonna be a hit!

C'mon, lighten up. Gimme a smile. That's my girl.

We oughta get goin' Beckaroo. Lots to do. Nah, lets take the ladder down from the window. Safe enough, I guess. Like we're escaping from a fire. And not for the first time either, I'll have you know. Just take a gander at these charred cheeks of mine. Kinda cool, don'tcha think? Yeah, well, I love what you did there to yourself. With your eyes I mean. Looking all charcoaled up like some raccoon. Really cool. Can't wait to hear your own story. The others are gonna love you; I can just tell. I'll go first. I promise not to look up your dress.

Gotta jump down at this last part, Becks. C'mon. S'okay. I'll catch you.

Oof!

Solid little gal, ain't ya! Hey, I'm just teasin'. I don't mean nuthin' by it.

C'mon, this way.

The muck out here in the backyard's a little hard to get through; gotta lift your legs up real high. That's right. You got it. It stinks pretty bad, I know. You'll get used to it, though. But you already got some gunk on that lovely lacey dress of yours. Ah well, not much to do about that. You already look a bit soiled anyway, if you don't mind my sayin'. On account of some girl? You don't say! Got even with her, did you? Oh yeah, I'm gonna wanna hear all about that one. Can't wait.

That's our big ol' barn up there just ahead. Gonna see if anyone else is hangin' about, if you don't mind.

Slip on through here, Becky. Easier than trying to open up that big ol' clunky barn door. Probably stuck that way forever, anyways. Watch your head, here. Kinda dark, but you'll get used to it in a sec'. Here, take my hand ... watch your head again, we're ducking under a stall ... there you go. C'mon out here in the middle of the big open area ... now look up toward all them cracks in the roof where the daylight is barely shinin' through ... do you see them? All them dark silhouettes, scads of 'em, hanging there from the rafters? All them bodies tied to ropes; all still-like. What? No, of course they're not real people. They're dummies. All dummies. Yeah, I know; too many to count, huh? Yeah, they're all dead. They can't talk about anything anymore. Just plain dumb. Get it? That one there, though ... you can't hardly see his face ... his head is bigger than the rest ... that's Clarence. He's the only one who ever makes a noise, but really he just moans. I guess he can't quite accept the fact that he's here with us now. It's like he keeps recalling back to when he was still alive.

Hey Schuster!

Yeah, I know, but Schuster's not a dummy. He just likes to hang around with them. I don't know why, Becks. Maybe he always dreamed of being someone else's mouthpiece. He won't tell me. But he's cool enough, I guess. Just that he seems to get a kick outta making Clarence miserable ... egging him on all the time; telling him vicious little stories to make him moan. I must admit, his moans can get pretty scary, 'specially at night. But Schuster, he just won't quit.

Hey Schust! This here's Becky. Miss Rebecca. She's a lady ... be nice.

Sorry Beck, Schuster's mouth gets a mite foul at times.

That's okay, Schust. We're gonna go ahead and mosey ourselves right along; head outside for a while. Maybe we'll come back later when you can shut that fucked-up pie-hole of yours. Sorry, sweetie. Let's head out back, through them old slaughtering pens ... you don't mind, do you? Just bones, hon. Just bones. Watch your step. Lookin' like it might rain down on us some time later on. 'Course, it always looks that way 'round here. Keeps everything dingy gray and gloomy. Dark clouds, dim forecast. You get the idea. You okay? You look a little ... I dunno ... pale. Those are some amazing cracks in your face, by the way. Jeezus, Beck, with a serving bowl? No shit? And your limp ... she did that too? Fuck me. Don't worry, you'll be taken care of here; I'll make damned sure of it.

Do you want to see our creek? It runs along over yonder there by them rotten tree trunks. We even got ourselves a tire swing ... do you believe it? C'mon, I'll give you a few shoves ... take your mind off your troubles.

Here, let me clean out some of this gunk in the tube first ... starts to build up after a while. Take care with your dress and hoist yourself up onto the hard-rubber rim. Perfect. You really are quite pretty, Becks. Just sayin'. Hold on now. Gonna shove you way out over the water. Okay ... that molten, wet brown sludge with the slow moving garbage in it ... but you gotta pretend, Becky ... you just gotta. Okay? That's a girl. Oh my god, did you just giggle? You should do it more, Becks. Quite becoming.

Okey doke, here we go then.

Hold on tight, sweets. I'm pretty strong.

Whoa! That was great, girl! You done sailed way, way out there. I thought you was gonna fly completely away from me. I got you now, though. Ready? This time, I'm gonna send you all the way up into them blustery storm clouds! Scare them damn black birds away, that's for sure. One, two three ...

Can you still hear me, Becks? Holy cow! You look like a lone angel flyin' up there all by yourself. A real lovely vision you're makin', too. Certainly gonna give that damned devil a run for his money.

One more time now ... hold on. Up we go!

Whoa! That was fun!

I gotcha now ... you can let go ... hey, this is kinda nice.

C'mon, I'll show you our windmills. You ain't tired, are you? Good.

Oh, I'm just lookin' up at them thick old clouds some more, Beck. Yeah, it's probably gonna rain any minute now. I know ... them birds is pickin' up, too ... but try not to worry yourself about them. They're not gonna get to you ... not yet ... not while I'm here. Worried? Naw, I ain't worried. That's just the way I sound sometimes. C'mon, let's get some shelter inside the big mill.

Sorry, not meanin' to rush you none ... but do try to keep up, okay?

Wup. Here it comes. We're gonna get soaked now, doll. Ain't no shelter between here and there, but we'll be okay. Take my hand and try not to slip. Ha!

Sorry. There goes your hair, I'm afraid.

We'll get ourselves dried off inside. I even got a little fireplace set up in the corner. I'll get some wood burnin' and you can get your dress off. Hey, I didn't mean it like that ... here's a blanket to cover you up. We just gotta get your clothes dry or you'll catch your death of pneumonia. Sorry, that's not all that funny, is it? Still, you'll be more comfortable when we do. C'mon over to the table here, Becks; have yourself a sit down. We've got a bit of talkin' to attend to. You're probably a tad confused, showin' up here so sudden-like. Frankly, and I really regret sayin' this ... you have no idea how much I do ... but I'm thinking maybe somebody made a big mistake. No, doll. Not you. I mean whoever's behind this miserable little town of ours. What I'm tempted to say is ... I'm not really sure that you should be here.

You don't quite fit.

Hold on. Hold on. Let me tell you a different story first.

I haven't always made my home here, you know. In fact, my name isn't really Chuck, either. It's Robert, but everybody calls me Chuck. That started when some bad things happened, things they said I did ... said I was always there at the time, lookin' on ... after which I came to be here. The name just kind of stuck with me after that. The others look at me like I'm some kind of hero for what I did, but it weren't me. It was Chuck. Still, what can I do? I'm here now, and it looks like I'm gonna be here most of forever ... either dead or dying, whatever this is we're doin'. And I musta did them things. I won't deny it. So I suppose I'm gonna pay for 'em. I don't mind too much, I guess. I'm sorta used to it by now. I got my friends ... Miles and Schust ... even Billie boy. But you, Beckaroo ... well, you see, I'm not truly convinced you're supposed to be here. No, I ain't sure of it at all. And though it tears me up to say this, I think maybe you won't be stayin' with us all that much longer.

I was hoping you could be my friend. I don't have a girlfriend, Becks, and I'm already liking you a lot. But them things that little girl did to you? Well, that weren't right of her. Not right at all. Though you were right to do what you done back to her. No, I'm absolutely sure of it. She's the one who should've been sent out here to join us ... but then again, she's real people ain't she ... she couldn't have ended up here anyway. But holy hell, we could've hung her up with all those other dummies and let Schust have his pitiful way with her. That would've been great. Just great.

Anyways, Becks, so here I am thinkin' that when the devil figures out just why you did them things ... not because you're bad, for goddssakes, but only to get your just desserts ... well, I'm afraid he's gonna send you back home. He's gonna take you away from me and send you someplace far away from this lovely little town of ours. I think he's gonna figure out you just ain't bad enough to be here.

Funny, huh?

So, whaddya think, Beck? You think maybe you could be bad? I mean, here and now be bad?

I know. I know. Kind of a strange thing to ask.

Still, ponder on it a bit, will ya? Cuz I sure would like it if you stayed.

Rain seems to be lettin' up at last ... your dress looks mostly dry ... wanna go out and play some more? Oh hey, I'm awful sorry. I didn't mean to make you cry. C'mon babe. I know, you're just confused. I shouldn'a said nuthin'. My big mouth. Always getting' me into so much trouble.

Let's go see Miles now. He's smarter'n I am. Maybe he can figure out what to do. We can ride them sails later.

Well jeez on me, Beck, lookit all them black birds. I never seen so many all at once. Stay close to me, hon ... and walk real slow. We gotta make our way 'round these crosses. You know, I ain't exactly sure who all's buried here. No, really. I ain't seen no buryin' been done since the day I first arrived. And them crosses look awfully old, even ancient. Maybe it was all them townsfolk who lived here before us. Maybe it was the real people. Wouldn't that just be somethin'. What a thought.

Let's cut across my yard to Miles' place.

We don't have to knock.

Hey Miles! You in there? Got someone for you to meet!

Maybe he's out back. Let's head on 'round the side.

Hey there Miles, whatchya up to'?

One foot ... good one.

This here's Becky ... Becky, Miles. Watch out for his strings, hon.

You know, Miles, I told you before. I can cut those things short anytime you want. Won't have to drag them through the mud like that. I know, I know ... it'd be kinda like cutting off all your hair, though what you got now looks sewn on anyway ... not like ol' Beck's genuine coiffure. Just a little joke, guy ... hey, take it easy, bud.

So sensitive.

Nuthin'. I didn't say nuthin'.

So Miles, we got us a little situation here maybe you can help us with. Here's the thing. I'm suspectin' our new little gal Becky ... maybe she ain't supposed to be in our nasty little town. I've listened to her tale, and she don't quite fit the profile, know what I mean? Not like you and me ... not like ornery ol'

Schuster with all his dummies. She ain't been bad ... not really. She only done what needed to be done when someone hurt her. Someone real. She weren't lookin' for no trouble. Not like us. I'm not sure the devil got this one figured out right.

What?

No, just the opposite. I want her to stay. I think she could learn to like it here. But she's gonna get found out and fly away. I don't want her to, Miles. I really don't. I was hopin' we could come up with somethin' really bad for her to do right here and now. Then they'd have to let her stay.

I like her, Miles. I want her to be happy.

Nuthin'? You got nuthin'? Here I was counting on you, Miles. No, it's okay. I was just really hoping we could do something nice for her. I guess we'll head on back to my place. Get her in from the cold. Try to figure somethin' out. You too, okay? Yeah, well thanks, bud.

C'mon, Becks.

Whoa! Holy shit! Where'd all them damn birds come from? I never seen nuthin' like it ... so many birds ... like they're blackin' out the whole damn sky ... darker than those ol' rain clouds, even. Oh man, Becks, you gotta get behind me now. Those birds are comin' for you. I can tell. They're gonna take you away from me, just like I said. I won't let 'em do it. I won't! Get yourself down on the ground, girl. Don't worry about your dress. Just hunker yourself down right here behind me.

Oh man, I got no weapon. Not even a stick.

You bloody fuckers! Leave my girl alone!

Wait! Hold on just a minute! Get your bloody talons off me! Aw cripes, Becky, I can't fight 'em off. What the bloody hell? What's happenin' to me? What're you doin' way down there, Rebecca? What're they doin' ... where are they taking me? Oh my god! Becky! They didn't come for you at all. They've come for me! I'm the one they're takin' away! It don't make no sense. I'm the one who done bad.

Can you hear me, Becks?

I'm sorry. Can you hear me? I'm so damned sorry. I didn't mean for you to stay there without me. Oh god, Becks, can you hear me! Go see Miles. Tell him to take good care of you for me. I'm gonna get back to you. I promise! Oh god, Becky, can you still hear me! I'm gonna do bad, Becky! I'm gonna do real bad for you. I'm gonna to the baddest thing of all!

Oh my sweet girl ... can you hear me?
Can you ...

*****

Hello there.

In our little town, I was told that the devil keeps his eye on us all.

Nothing but the dead and dying live here now.

I am one of them.

I'm Becky.

Maybe I can show you around a bit, give you the lay of the land, so to speak.

Don't mind the danger signs up ahead.

Or all them birds, either.

THE END

THE HANGING GIRLS

An old legend says that when you meet them in the woods, perhaps returning from a journey or leaving home to start one, a bad thing happens. That they represent a doorway into the darkness of another world, a world of such rude horror and neglect that one must leave his sanity behind in order to endure, perchance to manage an eventual escape. Such, at least, are the anecdotal ravings periodically handed down to us from bearded doctors as told to them by insane minds.

One such tale tells of little Marty Scrivener, a youth perhaps infused with too much imagination, his scrambled tattlings written down precisely and with achingly exquisite detail by that most prominent mental doctor of the early 1900's, one Ezekiel Bacon Berkshire. Dr. Berkshire did not come close to ascribing to young Scrivener's wide-ranging ramblings even a modicum of reality, but he was overtly eager to bestow upon this troubled youngster absolute credence regarding the intensity of his trials, and Marty was subsequently and professionally diagnosed with the simple psychiatric label: *a raving lunatic.*

Assuredly, he was not one when first he ventured into the woods. Not until he met the two hanging girls.

According to the good doctor's meticulous notes, Marty Scrivener's encounter with the girls proceeded blindly, and apparently unfortuitously, as the unplanned result of an inadvertent, random wandering into the woods. He was not leaving home, nor was he returning. He was simply walking about one autumn day and lost his way. Literally and figuratively; at least, psychologically speaking. And though his own narrative of subsequent events vibrated with the stridently disjointed symptoms of his diagnosed psychosis, one could almost hear the rationality of self-induced questioning that had preceded his dissolution. You could hear, even in the written replication of his tale, his desperate pleadings for coherence and belief.

"They was in their nighties, doc. Hanging from a tree."

And, when the doctor asked him to explain ...

"They was dead, doc. Both of 'em."

After that, the transcript gets a little rough, not because the doctor was less attentive, imprecise, or incomprehensive, but because the boy became more agitated and incoherent. What got written down and must therefore be accepted as a flawless reproduction, considering the doc's credentials, was a fragmented series of nightmarish images spouted forth as one might spew such epithets immediately upon waking from clinging night terrors.

"That dark cloud ... behind them ... spinning like a wheel.

"Those faces ... terrified ... staring at me ... eyes like boiling eggs.

"Screaming ... screaming ... hearing nothing.

"Scrawny hands ... reaching out ... grabbing at me.

"Pulling me in ... to be with them."

At this point, the doctor compassionately calls a break. He adds some preliminary speculative notations regarding a possible diagnosis with suggestive treatment, but for the moment they remain simple points on which to ponder later, and which in turn suggest that maybe our good Doctor Berkshire was simply stalling. Perhaps he too was rather shaken by the young fellow's authentic agitation. Perhaps, and this is only further speculation, privately he did hold a modicum of belief.

Doctor Berkshire allowed Marty's verbal ebullition to continue apace for quite a while, regrettably causing the youth much undue mental turmoil and *significantly irreversible psychic trauma* - the doctor's words for untold damage – though the doc himself would not acknowledge any professional complicity in bringing Marty down, nor in thus leaving him: *a raving lunatic in a vegetative state.*

One must be curious as to what Master Scrivener specifically had to say while ranting on about his terrible trials inside that cloud behind the girls, horrific as they must now be presumed. Alas, such curiosity must also remain unassuaged, as further recorded details were quietly redacted sometime in the recent past, at least within those records still open to public scrutiny under our modern *right-to-know* legal canons. We are left only to conjecture about what in particular might lead a young man toward such a total mental breakdown.

All of this, of course, precludes the more significant implications of the legend's origin itself. Where did the dead girls come from, and what horrible events led to their hanging dead together from a tree, dressed only in their nighties? That, in truth, is the matter of this story.

Delilah and Denise, twins of course, were born and raised as country girls back when the countryside was young. Raven-haired, but not quite beauties - it was difficult to tell since they had no access to enhancers – these two shared an inclination towards the cerebral side of life. Thinkers, not stinkers. Much of their mutual conversation was pre-intuited due to their genetic pairing, and thus they often skipped ahead to lounge languorously on the really good parts, filling gaps along the way with perhaps a single cogent word or two for traction.

Not so unexpectedly, considering the events that were yet to come, the twins early on developed a strange fondness for the ... *unusual*. Not to put too fine a point on it, the girls were fascinated, compulsively so, by thoughts about the supernatural. From where such an obsessive predilection originated, only a trained psychologist might propose, but the fact remains: the girls spent an inordinate amount of time and conversation exploring the theoretical phenomena of supernatural things.

Naturally, in time, their interest turned from speculation to exploration. And naturally, non-theoretically, things went straight to hell.

Their delving into matters most *unusual* occurred, appropriately enough, in a manner most unusual. The girls had not learned anything about the supernatural aspects of the world through reading. As mentioned, Delilah and Denise were raised in the countryside, at a time when books were not nearly so widespread, and certainly before the supernatural itself became something of a popular item for an increasingly indulgent, greedy public. The girls ate their own portions of the weird as if they had magically conjured up a variety of pastries strictly suited to their tastes – doling out to one another the minor delicacies they had created.

That is to say: they pretty much made stuff up.

No one had told them they could not.

By the time the twins had reached their teenage years, they no longer saw anything extraordinary about their co-creations, and certainly nothing to inspire distaste or that which they should fear. They were lulled into an almost indifferent acceptance of what they together conjured up, things that would frighten those bound unto the real world, but which to them appeared more like necessary companions in a very lonely life, especially after Mom and Dad spontaneously disappeared. The philosophical problems embedded in creating one's own reality was magnified automatically by two, but were also expanded by the concomitant reality that the girls had no clue at all as to what they had been doing. Such was the nature of their childhood; such was the nature of their teenage years.

In truth, they had been opening up another world.

As Delilah and Denise – always Delilah first, for she was the older by a minute – explored the culinary delights of the unusual, their appetites remained slightly unappeased. A certain something seemed always to be lacking. The perfect dessert, perhaps, to stretch the metaphor to its limit. This led to their preliminary expedition deep into the woods that completely surrounded their country home. They sensed something out there waiting, something they could use to make their meals even more satisfying. Their sense for such had been well-honed in childhood, and the teens were quite confident they could find that for which they searched – something on which to better focus their attention, something sweet, something to make their conjurings more worthwhile.

Our girls were delighted and entranced by the unusual spot they found. The darkness could not be seen, but they felt it so strongly inside their bones that they simply vibrated with the intensity of an energy sizzling all around them, as if the air were totally electrified or the earth engulfed in flames, but with electricity that was midnight black and flames born of ebony, so strong the girls could see the roiling, spinning hole inside their heads, and from this alone a great conjuring could be had.

The big question, asked first by young Denise, became: "What shall we do with this?"

Upon which older Delilah pondered, answering, "Like a gift, we open it."

Which made the girls grin as they went nonchalantly about their business.

That evening, while lying in their beds, trying to drift toward sleep, they talked about the incredibly *unusual* thing they had gone ahead and conjured up, and then what they had incredulously witnessed there inside it.

"Did you see those awful people?" asked Denise, rhetorically.

"Gruesome," answered Delilah.

"Their boiling eyes ... "

"Their scrawny hands ... "

"Their terrible, screaming faces," they said together.

The girls shivered with delight. Dessert, indeed. They would not go to sleep still hungry on this fine, culminative night. And yet, just a little something still pricked at them, something that seemed to say in a voice deep with possible foretelling and yet also titillating with dreadful teasing, "All is not yet done."

With that the girls sighed, and mostly satisfied, they turned onto their tummies and went to sleep.

Still in their nighties early the next morning, they decided to venture back into the woods to see the darkly spinning hole. They found the right spot easily enough, but they were chagrined not to find the hole still positioned there, though its ecstatic energy remained as present and strong as ever.

"I guess we've got to open it again," said Delilah.

"I guess so," Denise agreed.

Which they accomplished with no great effort, but even though the screaming people with boiling eyes and scrawny, bony hands reappeared as summoned, the girls realized they had also created for themselves a minor problem. They did not wish to re-open the same hole every day, not because of any unduly strenuous effort, but simply because the repetitive act itself would become quite boring. They suspected, too, that sitting there just watching those freakish people suffer inside the hole, no matter how vivid it might remain, could still become repetitious, and therefore not unusual, wherein lay the crux of their minor problem: they could not risk losing contact with such superlative potential.

That night, still dressed in their same nighties and once again in bed, they discussed it further.

"I've been thinking," began Delilah.

"About our minor problem," Denise continued.
"Keeping the hole open."
"Without it becoming boring."
"Exactly."

And then, unexpectedly for the twins because they had become routinely proficient in their shared ability to mutually please themselves, Delilah individually sparked a new idea for expanding their joy and possible entertainment.

"We can open up the door, that's what it is, and lodge it open for all time."

Denise did not immediately catch on.

"What would be unusual about that?"

"We could watch others find it for the first time."

"Others," Denise murmured, as if contemplating something foreign.

"What others?" she asked, at last.

"Anyone else who ventures by," Delilah said.

"But, no one ever ventures by," Denise remarked.

Delilah smiled slyly when she responded.

"Yes, but we could make them," she said.

A new sensation infused them both upon reflection, something quite salacious, savory, and erotic.

Once again, the girls smiled, turned over, and went to sleep.

Early morning found them still wearing their old nighties, now beginning to show serious signs of soiling from two days spent idling in the woods watching tormented people scream and writhe, a source of no little curiosity and satisfaction to the twins.

Now they stood thoughtfully in their front yard.

Denise, consistently a minute behind her sister, asked, "How do we lodge that dark door open?"

Delilah answered, "We're going to need some rope."

Being country girls, they quickly acquired precisely what they needed.

Then they headed for the woods.

You might rightly wonder at the thing they did next to permanently keep propped open that hellish door, but the girls had first to hang themselves. They knew this to be true, the same way when they were young they knew how to conjure up poltergeists and demons. The knack was already in their genes.

Delilah and Denise trussed themselves up quickly before shimmying up the tree nearest to the hole, tying off the rope ends tightly and securing them to one large branch, and without much hesitation after opening up the door, they both prepared to make their final jump.

"Love you," said Delilah to Denise, and leapt.

Denise would follow Delilah one minute later.

The sister thing allowed her to find delight in Delilah's lengthy strangulation before going completely still. Basked in the pleasure of her own anticipation, Denise then jumped too.

In throes of their own agony, the people inside the hole looked aghast at the two still girls now hanging just outside.

Where the girls would stay, looking dejected, depressed, and dead.

Which they were not.

Not quite.

Perforce, in order to clarify such a non-intuitive conclusion to this unusual set of deeds, one more story must be told.

Although others did eventually pass by as forecast by Delilah, seemingly through unprovoked happenstance, which it was not, none confirmed the forewarnings put forth later in the legend more than Mary Rogers, a middle-aged spinster from Missouri, who for inexplicable reasons one day found herself lost and wandering in the woods.

Yes, those woods.

We know of Mary Rogers from her psychiatric history recorded at the local equivalent of old Bellevue, records that resonate unquestionably with those of young Marty Scrivener, omitting the addition of a crucial revelation given freely to her doctor – not the famous one – in which the vital missing piece, if one were to lend full credence to the legend, makes for rather an elegant completion of this enigmatic puzzle.

Like Marty, Mary could not adequately explain why or how she came to be wandering in those woods, but she did admit to once hearing the strangest story of a crazy boy who once-upon-a-time had done the same thing. She could not remember any details, though in the agitated state in which she began her recitation, calmed only when driven to hypnosis, she was unlikely to have been coherent anyway, either about her recent memories or her personal rationale for being there. Those memories remained lucid under trance, but were filled with terrifying recollections, which were conveyed with disarmingly excessive precision under the calming effects of her hypnosis, including important details describing what she had seen inside the hole.

Perhaps this part of the story we should let her tell in her own words.

"I don't know what I was doing there," she says, in a monotonously hypnotic voice, actually recorded and available for anyone to hear. "I guess I wanted to be alone. I felt lost and a bit unnerved, but not afraid. It was shady in the woods. And cool. No breeze, but still nice. Kind of peaceful, I guess you'd say.

"I don't know how long I walked about, but the more I walked, the less I seemed to care about my being lost, though I did feel anxious, like I said. Maybe at my own absence of concern. I don't know. I feel so calm right now. Not so much, back then. The air begin to thicken. Funny how I remember that. It happened just before I saw the two dead girls hanging from the tree. I knew they were dead, and I got scared. They looked ... I don't know ... like they had been hanging there such a long time. So distressed. There was a darkness just behind them. Not darkness all around. Just darkness spinning in a circle right behind them.

"I went to look. I had to. I couldn't help it.

"I went behind the girls and looked into the empty dark. But it wasn't empty. I saw awful, screaming faces. Horrible disfigured faces, in paralyzing agony. Eyes churning like eggs in boiling water. And hands reaching out for me ... grasping me like demonic skeletons ... drawing me toward them ... dragging me inside."

Mary should have screamed, but her throat was too constricted.

"The horror was ... indescribable. No words. Knowing only that suffering is eternal. And meant for all. With no way out."

A pause of lengthy silence before she offers an enticing tidbit.

"But ... I found a way."

Mary, in her last reflective moment, then proffers her final pièce de résistance.

"I saw the same two girls inside, grinning back at me."

Unfortunately, the deceptive calmness with which Mary tells her story completely dissipates upon waking from her trance, and no amount of post-hypnotic suggestion could eradicate the lasting effects of her experience. Mary's doctor prescribed strong medication to subdue her ravings, but left the woman two options only: face the haunting nightmares found in sleep, or face the haunted ones of waking.

Either choice was hell.

Such anecdotal research reveals no inconsistency in other stories such as Mary's. One might say, a plethora of them now exist. But anecdotal revelations, no matter how prolific, bear no weight with professionals or academics.

Therefore, the stories must continue as legend only.

Quite old, but most *unusual*, to be sure.

*****

An addendum to the old legend of the hanging girls.

Something should have been conveyed to you prior to your reading, and it is criminal that it was not. There is an undeniable corollary attendant to your hearing of this legend.

You see, our girls did not just eternally lodge the door open.

Nor did they fully decease themselves in so doing.

Remember, their last conjuring act among the normal living was to guarantee there would be visitors to watch from within their newly created situation, by which they would possess eternal delight and satisfaction.

That should be obvious.

But, the manner in which they procured this guarantee might still elude you.

It is quite simple, though.

By invoking the proper incantatory invocations prior to their jumping, our two hanging girls insured that whoever listened to the future legend – intentionally or not – would afterward venture into those woods alone. Everything after that was preordained. Nasty, but there was only one way not to mingle with the screamers.

One way to evade their grasping claws.

One way to escape their particular, eternal suffering.

Dr. Berkshire said it best.

109

And now, it will soon apply to you.

THE END

THE HANGED MAN

The sky is such a gray it looks purple.
Dark and purple.
And wet.

The cobblestoned street shines with wet. A recent rain has left it glistening with random patches of pooled water. The non-descript village looks like something risen from the dark ages, the main street wide enough for horse-drawn carts, the buildings close-packed and built of stones, and where the street ends a stony spire rises up from an old church steeple or castle tower obscured by the pall of purple gray. A flock of black birds silhouetted in the waning sky accentuates the abandoned situation of this deserted town, drawing one's attention to the hanged man, also silhouetted, with arms lashed crucifixion-style to a ship's reclaimed yardarm projecting high above the empty street from a nearby clay-tiled roof.

Despite this obviously inauspicious warning, one is drawn to walk on past the darkened doorways, past the boarded-up, iron-trellised windows, past the occasional unlit, isolated street lamp – single mourners for the town – remaining hushed and thoughtful and mentally abraded by a disquieted but nagging curiosity that insistently demands: what has happened here? The jealous, eerie silence holds possessively to its unforthcoming answers, as do the softly plinking drops still falling intermittently from all the building's corniced eaves into designated puddles just beneath. The figure of the hanged man retreats inexorably behind the curious walker, now an inadvertent intruder into this recently vanquished town, feeling the not-long-dead eyes of crucifixion boring deeply into his exposed and tingling neck. He feels vulnerable, but he does not look back at what is making so many fine skitterings shudder down his spine.

He already knows.

The steepled tower that looms so righteously above the long street's final ending belongs to a minor-ranked cathedral, something our reluctant walker notes while approaching ever more closely, but even this impressive stone-wrought building with its darkly shadowed, forbidding windows looks to be utterly abandoned and totally inaccessible, no longer a likely sanctuary from whatever cruel malignancy earlier befell this blighted town. Still, one feels unusually compelled to investigate further because of a niggling and tenaciously lingering doubt about what might transpire inside, and the walker therefore proceeds halfheartedly up to the heavy wooden alcove door - lashed with steel bandings and cone-curved at the top – a door that looks freakishly miniature in relation to the whole structure, as if it had been cut by human mice to block a secretive little entry hole.

The door remains ajar, only slightly, but enough to push it open and thereby initiate a quiet entrance. A drafty stone-built hallway greets our bold intruder, beckoning him toward a single source of flickering light coming from a waning torch ensconced within a metal-banded holder bolted to an obstructing wall marking the hallway's end. The shadowy, agitated eeriness caused by the torch flame's inability to get enough necessary air lends a feeling of haunted reverence to the corridor's appearance, suggesting once again a warning against proceeding any farther; a warning once again ignored.

The corridor branches to the left and leads down a narrow flight of wooden stairs. The awkwardly dancing light behind gives some illumination to the over-worn steps ahead, but there is also the barest impression of more light yet to come suggested by an oddly bluish glow emanating upward from the bottom. The stairs will surely creak, they always do, but there is also a softly thrumming sound issuing up from somewhere down below, perhaps enough to mute the sound of someone's uninvited passage.

The walker descends.

The diminished lighting, oddly enough, comes from a single candle burning down into oblivion within its small brass holder - shaped like a flat round tea saucer properly adorned with one convenient finger loop – sitting on a much too messy wooden desk. Its already dissipated form – a brain-like mass of melted wax overspilling the tarnished metal circle - hastens to absorb what little life remains to burn, suggesting an all-too-brief reprieve from utter darkness. The eerie glow, however, comes not from this unwaxing candle, but from a knee-high flood of ambient, bluish fog that looks suspiciously like those undulating waves of noxious marsh gas found so often haunting remote and uninviting swamps. The room is flooded, permeated with this strange effluence. The floor cannot be seen. One must necessarily choose to descend no farther.

"I would not choose to step there," comes a raspy voice out of darkness.

In a far corner of this flooded basement repository sits a two-story bed called a bunk, on top of which sits an emaciated man, or at least the hint of one observed, but only as a human-figured opaqueness against the dimly lit wall just behind him. He sits cross-legged with his back against the wall. And though the stone surfaces around him appear to be flickering themselves into life, the mealy man's silhouette does not. He merely looks to be crumbling into place, just like the candle stub incessantly succumbing unto itself.

He too could rightly accuse himself of melting down.

"Come no farther," the voice repeats. "Though for you it may be too late."

A brutal hacking cough erupts from the man's pathetically inadequate frame, making him jerk suddenly like a spastic marionette controlled by an epileptic puppeteer. And even as he then puddles calmly down onto the bed, the candle sitting on his long avoided messy desk abides unto itself, the flame flickers thrice and dies.

The idle walker stands, and making his way back up the stairs, he leaves.

Up above, back outside the stone cathedral, the day has inevitably turned blustery with cold. Old shutters shake and rattle, wisps of water fling themselves in outward fanning sprays against another building's wall, while dark leaves like blackbird wings flit spasmodically across the sky, looking like the dancers in some macabre, sinful celebration. The walker simply hunkers down and proceeds beyond the overbearing cathedral to where the villager's quaint and unpretentious homes are huddled like frightened children left together after dark.

Beneath the purple storm clouds and dismal fading skies, the houses resemble empty darkened boxes. No lanterns hang inside the windows to beckon passing strangers, no glow of fireplace creates a warm, familiar scene, no sound of little voices playing, nor older ones discussing.

All is dead.

Muddy alleys run between the crowded neighborhood blocks, portending only doom should one choose to venture down one.

Yet, a shuffling sound - coming from what looks to be a tumbled down trash mound piled loosely at the end of a particularly lonesome looking alley - begs for such investigation, as any singular sign of life now becomes a homeless vagrant pleading for an individual need. Our walker makes his way slowly down this otherwise empty corridor of stone and wet to see what lies waiting restlessly in the sodden heap of trash. Most of the old garbage is already covered with wayward leaves blown here by the wind, captured by the gravitational pull of such a mordant mass, and layered on until the pile resembles nothing less than a formidable mountain of accumulated muck.

Perhaps that is what attracted this creature into such a murky mound's uncomfortable embrace – it seems like an entirely appropriate place to die.

Which is precisely what this mostly unidentifiable animal is near the completion of doing for itself. The only discernible characteristic defining it as a living being, though certainly one not human, is the flickering light of one small eyeball left gazing upward at the watcher as if to appreciate the witnessing of this final, sacrificial, sacred rite. And even as this faint glimmer fades toward that milky opaqueness attributable to death, a squeak reminiscent of a hungry kitten issues from the rigor of its open mouth, where sharpened little teeth speak of a more glorious personal, predatory history.

What was surely once a cat now slips quietly into its death with a most inglorious demise.

The walker steps away from the blue phosphorescent puddle spreading listlessly across the ground, careful not to touch anything in his path, and he warily and shamefully retreats from this broken alley that had seemed so despairingly to be calling out his name.

The day has turned to darker purple, evening now departing for the rapid fall of night. The cold seems also to have turned more severe. Neither overly daunts our walker, though he does have the forlorn appearance throughout his purposeful if aimless strides of one hunched over and leaning forward, as if everything he might be looking for still lies somewhere up ahead, or like those mysteriously cloaked strangers on city streets who hunch their shoulders just the same in order to insistently forge themselves forward against a blustery, driving rain.

As if in answer to this sodden image, the rain begins to fall again.

The road becomes muddy leading out of town.

In resonance with the basement room in the cathedral and the quivering shadow in the alley, far off in the distance, beneath the opaquely darkened silhouettes provided by an expansive grove of trees - perhaps a cultivated orchard bearing fruit - a flickering yellow flame suggests a local fire with oddly gesticulating figures grouped protectively around, obviously come together for congeniality and warmth.

A gathering place for the few survivors from whatever befell their now abandoned town.

The low murmuring buzz of human interaction and conversation disturbs the evening air, drawing the would-be observer closer toward the possibility of companionship and contact. And yet, instinctively, he stops and waits beyond the rim of firelight in order just to listen and to learn what may be told by way of revelation. The voices are not fearful, nor are they strident. They are not engaged in long harangues of disagreement. Though some figures move fretfully around the fire, poking sticks into the bed of embers, idly pushing ashes into mounds, the others sit less active, simply watching. These are the ones who murmur to each other with the kind of quiet thoughtfulness brought on by deep fatigue, a weariness often born of hopelessness and helplessness.

The kind filled with deep regret.

The kind shared by huddled refugees.

The kind that breeds a reluctant storyteller born to fill an eerie quiet.

Except that some stories, like this story, are not about some wondrous beings who happenstance brought together once upon a time, long ago, and far away. The listeners gathered here, looking war-torn and traumatized, are fidgety and anxious to understand what happened just today, this day so woefully begun and only now just passed away, in this their normally uneventful, thoroughly un-wondrous - and to them most unremarkable - little town.

"It was the stranger," our designated storyteller begins, not with the vile accusatory tone normally reserved for shunned outsiders, but with the resignation heard inside the necessary observation of one's final submission to acceptance. "We should not have let him in."

"Aye," is heard from several other voices.

"But we did not know better," the teller continues, apologetic for them all.

"He looked okay, if perhaps a little weary. I watched him from the window of my shop. He came walking into town like so many others have. Horseless. Cartless. A leather satchel strapped down across his shoulder, as if he might have money left to spend. A dirty hat to shade his face. Just a weary traveler. That is all he seemed to be."

The speaker ponders the non-accountability registered in his voice, picks up a stick to doodle idly in the dirt, as if this inane distraction might discredit any accusatory admonitions from the rest. For their part, they are simply waiting to hear more, caught up in their own guilty responsibility for still surviving, hoping to find a rationale within the speaker's words for putting this all behind them. Tomorrow, they may move on, with just another story to be told and another left far behind.

Of course, they cannot resist a furtive glance back into their deserted town.

They do not, however, see the one who sits a short way off, alone, apart, and watching.

Listening so intently.

"I thought he must be okay when he stopped to pet the cat. That old scruffy stray didn't take to many people, so I thought ... this guy must be okay." The speaker shakes his head, knowing he over-repeats that word "okay," but there is a repetitious mantra running through his head insisting, "I'm okay. I'm okay."

He knows that he is not.

While he succumbs to his inner turmoil, another voice speaks up from elsewhere in the group.

"He wanted directions to the preacher man, but I thought how obvious that should be. Not like the church has made itself obscure. And I watched my friend across the way point his finger toward the steeple and then wave at the guy to be on about his business."

This new speaker also lapses into silence quickly, losing himself in those obtrusive thoughts prompted by his innocuous recollection.

A lady's voice enters the discussion next, bearing with it an unavoidable hint of blame, though centered on the stranger and not on those around her.

"That danged cat slithered past me on its way into an alley." Her words are bloated with disgust, which she moves to disgorge swiftly. "It was trailing its ...," and here she cackles with the cleverness of her wit, "its entrails behind itself like some kind of umbilical cord connected to the devil." Whereupon she spits and crosses herself and figures she best shut up about such hellish matters. She does not mention the phosphorescent blueness she saw coming from the cat. She is not even sure she remembers that part correctly.

"I haven't seen the preacher man," a small voice mentions. "Not since all those people started falling."

This shuts up the entire group as each head silhouetted before the flames begins to run a horrible sequence of events through its over stressed, distressed brain, a sequence shuffled like a pack of pictures at a fair, where such a shuffling creates the illusion of disarticulated movement, like a marionette or an ancient demon made to dance his demonic dance, usually around a fire just like this one. Each one sees a friend or loved one falling down to earth, caught up in random spastic motions like some demented victim suffering a bout of idiocy, their mouth stretched tight in a premature rictus that makes them grin like one suddenly possessed by too many strange delights.

The people fidget and they fuss, disturbed by this burdensome intrusion on their silence.

Some steal a backward glance toward town, as if the fallings might still be taking place.

At this precise moment, one old crone who has not yet spoken, rises from her place before the fire, stares piercingly into the darkness, shielding her fiercely searching eyes as if smitten by the sun, and crossing herself vigorously across her bony chest she makes her way hunched forward toward the darker spot within the outer darkness where our walker waits and watches quietly but listens with unduly attentive ears. The old lady points a gnarled finger directly at the implication of his presence and screeches out a curse.

"Be gone, ye devil not a man. Be gone. I put the curse o' God upon ye!"

When she spits upon the ground, the others stare horrified at the emptiness she is addressing. But they feel the sudden faint breeze of hurried flight, and they think they hear the fluttering of velvet wings retreating.

In his hurried flight backwards into town, the curiosity of the walking man has been subdued, his over-riding question – what happened here? - has been most adequately answered. His memory of his own recent past has been restored just like his curse, and he now recalls with full clarity the mass of falling people, the spastic twitching fits, the lengths of appalling, smelly, trailing entrails, and most of all, the constant haze of phosphorescent blue. But these recollections are in reality from a different town, one a lot like this one to be sure, a village plucked from the dark ages, where a stranger once came walking into town, boldly, blithely wandering through, but leaving behind himself a terrible legacy, a woeful tale of misery and death and phosphorescent blue. His personal contagion of the spirit became his affliction, the affliction became diseased, and the disease portended death for anyone whose path he crossed.

Invading and occupying all inhabitants of the village, animal or not.

The fallings and the dyings and the leavings.

The useless, final tales spoken listlessly around the fires.

With such potently vile reminiscings, the walker flies backward through the night, thinking that he feels the briskly fleeting air upon his skin, though he is skinless; fearing he might crash into a buttress or a stone-built wall, though he has no body which to crash. He is but the essence of a phosphorescent blue, taking flight across the night, back to where he has been cursed to hang forever, back where the villagers in their fright and judication have assigned all blame to him - the stranger in their midst.

The walker flies backward to his earlier crucifixion.

He now hangs motionless from the yardarm once again, with his arms still firmly bound and far outstretched, his shoulders crudely broken, his head hung low in shame.

He faces the cathedral where the preacher man endured his own shameful dissolution.

Past the alley where the homeless cat transformed itself to rancid trash.

Into the purpled night where he cannot see the massive flight of blackbirds passing far above and beyond this desolated, devastated town.

All is quiet now in the village.

No more plinking drops of rain.

No more windy flights of leaves.

All remains dead and still.

Until the hanged man's eyes open, and he chuckles mirthlessly at his fate.

THE END

AFTERWORD

www.amazon.com/Joel-R.-Dennstedt

PLEASE POST AN AMAZON REVIEW

As an Independent Author, the best way to gain an audience of happy readers is for my current readers to post their honest rankings and reviews on Amazon.

When Dolls Talk took more than one year to complete. Each story is based upon a creepy or ghoulish photograph found on the Internet and shared on my Facebook Author Page. Based upon such dramatic motivations, I let my imagination loose to play.

This book was the result.

As a non-stop world-trekker with every possession in a backpack and a duffel, I share my ongoing adventures and writing updates in my monthly Newsletter. I would love to have you join me.

NEWSLETTER:
http://eepurl.com/bUWg_f

ACKNOWLEDGEMENTS

One might think an Indie Author would have no one to acknowledge but himself. After all, he writes, he edits, he proofreads, he publishes, he markets and he sells. All by himself.

But he does not do this in a vacuum.

This book is dedicated to my three British author fans.

We are in this struggle together, and they have been most supportive. Glynis Heathcote, Chantelle Atkins, Steph Gravell. Thank you for always reading, encouraging, and faithfully sharing with your friends and followers.

Tom Hoffman is an accomplished graphic artist and the author of several exquisitely charming books about adventurous mice and rabbits – books not only for the young. Thank you for your gracious contributions to my books, especially this one.

Most importantly of all, I must thank you, the reader. As an avid reader myself, I know we often feel invisible and unknown to the authors of the books we read. Our favorite authors remain distant and inaccessible. We feign to understand, but what we want most is one intimate conversation. Please know, sometimes that is what we want, too.

These are the people I must acknowledge for motivating me to write this book and to make it better, and I thank them deeply for their support.

Joel R. Dennstedt – March 2017

www.joelrdennstedt.com
www.facebook.com/JoelRDennstedt

OTHER WRITINGS

GUANJO – A SCIENCE FICTION NOVEL
(2015)

HERMIT – A NOVEL
(2014)

ORANGE CAPPUCCINO – A NOVEL
(2012)

Made in the USA
Lexington, KY
08 March 2018